LIBRARY
FOR THE
WAR-
WOUNDED

A NOVEL

MONIKA HELFER

Translated by GILLIAN DAVIDSON

BLOOMSBURY PUBLISHING

NEW YORK · LONDON · OXFORD · NEW DELHI · SYDNEY

BLOOMSBURY PUBLISHING
Bloomsbury Publishing Inc.
1385 Broadway, New York, NY 10018, USA

BLOOMSBURY, BLOOMSBURY PUBLISHING, and the Diana logo
are trademarks of Bloomsbury Publishing Plc

First published in 2021 in Germany as *Vati* by Carl Hanser Verlag
First published in the United States 2024

Copyright © Monika Helfer, 2024
Translation © Gillian Davidson, 2024

ISBN: HB: 978-1-63973-239-5; EBOOK: 978-1-63973-240-1

Library of Congress Cataloging-in-Publication Data is available.

2 4 6 8 10 9 7 5 3 1

Typeset by Integra Software Services Pvt. Ltd.
Printed and bound in the U.S.A.

To find out more about our authors and books visit www.bloomsbury.com
and sign up for our newsletters.

Bloomsbury books may be purchased for business or promotional use.
For information on bulk purchases please contact Macmillan Corporate
and Premium Sales Department at specialmarkets@macmillan.com.

für meine Bagage
for my Bagage

We called him *Vati*, Dad. That's what he wanted. Vati, not Papa. He thought it sounded modern. He wanted to present himself to us, and through us, as a man in tune with the modern age. A man who could be read as having a different past. During the day and at night too, I think about him, sitting in his armchair under the standing lamp, children all around him, his own and some from other families, like the ones from the ground floor. Their ball rolls around his feet, under the chair, he is unconcerned. He is reading.

In the photograph that I have stuck to the wall above my desk, he is standing on the left, slightly apart. He looks as if he doesn't belong there. In all the other photos that my stepmother has shown me, our father stands right in the centre of the group, our real mother at his side; that was only proper, he was the host, the manager of the Convalescent Home for War-wounded on the Tschengla Plateau in the Austrian Alps, 1,220 metres above sea level. In most of the photos he is smiling. Not in the photo above my desk. My sister Gretel and I are standing at the front beside our mother. She is resting her hands on our shoulders. No one would guess that the man standing off to the left is our father. He looks like a man from the city who has attached himself to the group. As if one of them has said: come on, squeeze in here! Among the others some are definitely city folk, probably even the majority, but they have dressed like locals, in traditional jackets with horn buttons, sturdy ankle boots – although it's summer. I am sure they would have loved to have been locals. For this was paradise. The meadows full of the most brightly coloured flowers. I could name them all.

In the nineties – by then I had four children myself – I had travelled with him from Austria to Berlin to visit my sister Renate. It was his idea. I was not so keen. I feared it would be embarrassing. That he would open up about some dark secret or other, would tell me something about himself. I would have found anything embarrassing, even the most banal story. When you know a person your whole life and don't discover who they really are until late in the day, coming to terms with that may be difficult. It was already midnight when we arrived. The trains had been running almost two and a half hours late, there was no dining car, we were exhausted and hungry. Renate had not laid in any supplies because she was counting on us going out for a good meal. Now most of the restaurants in the area had closed, apart from one opposite her house: a gay bar where they served good food and didn't have loud music, something our father really couldn't stand. We ordered sauerkraut and some tender meat that looked a bit grey, and then he signalled to the waiter to come over and asked him: 'Where is the little girls' room?' Outbursts of laughter in the restaurant. He enjoyed that. When he came back from the toilet, his back bent over, limping, he sat himself down beside the men with make-up on their faces, with their sleeve-less vests and muscly, tattooed upper arms, and they treated him to a few glasses of schnapps and drank to his health. He was the smallest of them all, a dull grey figure among colourful birds. They laughed, and he laughed with them. They were not laughing *at* him; they just felt like laughing, and he too just felt like laughing at the end of this exhausting day. He no longer took any notice of my sister and me. We could hear him speaking in a tone of voice that we had not heard from him before, loud and clear; usually he sort of muttered to himself, you often had to ask him to repeat what he had said. One of the men came over to our table and said: 'Please come and join us. Your father is quite a character, really a character, we're getting on like a house on fire.' I remembered this word for word and Renate did too. By this he meant – this was our interpretation afterwards – that our father, who seemed such a dull grey man, like a government official, which is what in fact he was, and what's more, a tax department official, that our father was in reality a colourful personality. When Renate and I remember this, we can't help laughing out loud – as loud as he laughed. My husband says, whenever you two laugh like that it's because you're reliving what your father was like in Berlin. I say: 'You're spot on.'

The photograph above my desk was given to me by my stepmother. When I paid her a visit, our father had already been dead for ten years and she herself was over eighty.

I said: 'Could you spare me some time?'

'How long?' she asked.

'Quite long.'

'So this is about your father,' she said, 'isn't it?'

'I want to write a novel about him.'

'True or made-up?'

I said: 'Both, but more true than made-up. Would you have something?'

She: 'Wait until I'm dead. Then it can't upset me.'

She went up to the next floor and came back down with a large folder. Inside were about ten photographs, each one enlarged to the size of a school notebook. She pushed her ashtray and the bottle of Maggi sauce to one side and laid the pictures on the kitchen table. My older sister Gretel and I were in all of them.

'These are from Erwin Thurnher,' she said. 'He sent me them a while back.'

'Who's he?' I asked.

'You must know who he is! The photographer who took the pictures of you all at the Tschengla. At the end of each session.'

I remembered the man. Always dashing about. It had been exciting each time he'd set up his tripod and given his instructions.

'What's the story behind this photo?' I asked. 'This one here. Why is Vati not standing beside us?'

'You tell me,' she said. 'I wasn't even there. I didn't even know him then. Look at him! What's he thinking right now? That he might start studying again after all? Or maybe not? That he might make something of his life? Or that he can never make something out of his life, ever? Or that perhaps everything will come good in the end? Or maybe not? That all he dreamed of has come to naught? That everything is over? This time for good? That he'll push you all, his wife and his children, into the abyss? That he'll end up in the abyss himself? Everything over, gone? That he no longer wants to live? Because he doesn't want to be there when everything is over for all of you too …'

'Stop it!' I cry out. 'You can't see from a photo what someone's thinking!'

'If you know what someone's thinking, you can see it in their face,' she said.

5

'Not in his face,' I said. 'No one could ever see anything in his face.'

He was smaller than all the other boys, and none of the other boys ever knew where they stood with him, and so they didn't let him play with them. They were small, too, smaller than the young louts from the town, but they were taller than him and stockier. He was delicate. And pale-skinned. No red cheeks. No colour at all in his face. Slightly narrow eyes. And black hair. Pure white skin. Like a girl. No one made fun of him. Even as a child my father was a person who commanded respect. I suspect that this was because he always spoke calmly. If someone speaks calmly, people assume that they see no reason to get hot and bothered. People like that. That's why everyone liked my father. But when the boys were planning some mischief – and in the country play-ing always counts as mischief – they didn't want him tagging along. Because they were afraid he would say what they were up to was mischief. Everything gets its label after the fact – what childhood is, or complexity, mischief, peace, dissembling …

Even the poorest family was better off than my father and his mother. She was the housemaid of a farmer in Lungau. And unmarried. She had two outfits: one for everyday wear – dress, apron, stock-ings, shirt, underclothes – and one for Sundays. Just like most other people. The Sunday outfit though did not belong to her. It was on loan from the farmer's wife. On permanent loan to be exact, but nevertheless on loan. There were some household items on permanent loan too – crockery, a lampshade, a copper pan, I can't list them all, don't even know what they all were. On loan meant simply: it does not belong to you. What belonged to her outright was pretty much nothing. The father of her boy was the farmer. That was neither admitted nor contested. So her boy, too, was only half hers. We never spoke about this at home. My father would have rebuffed attempts. He did not want to be reminded of this time. If it had been acknowledged formally that the farmer was his father, he would probably have addressed him in the Tyrolean way as '*Date*'. He was spared that. So he was able to keep out of the farmer's way without appearing ungrateful. Of activities like dancing or singing or swimming or drama, my father used to say: 'Fortunately I was spared that.' It makes him sound like a misanthrope. He wasn't though.

My sister Gretel drove once to Mariapfarr in the Lungau region of Salzburg – she is interested in family history and ancestry. She wanted to see where our father grew up. Not that she wanted to establish lasting contact with anyone in particular. She just felt it was something one should know about. By that time, our father's mother was no longer alive. But her blind sister was still alive, the kindly Aunt Genoveva, known as Vev. Our father did not know that Gretel was digging into his origins. He would not have been happy about it. Aunt Vev now lived in the farmhouse and was almost one hundred. The farmer's son, who rented rooms to summer visitors, had a big heart or rather he did what any decent person would do; it was a large house, and he'd had one room under the roof refurbished for Aunt Vev. A large porcelain bowl stood on a chest of drawers, beside it a jug and a soap dish in the same pattern; these already took up half the room. She carried the water up herself. Her body smelled of hard soap, her hair too. Gretel said that Aunt Vev would sit every morning on her bed and brush her hair. Her hair ran right down to her bottom. She would brush her hair one hundred times, she would count each stroke. She was called 'our friendly ghost' by the farmer's son and his wife, for she was always everywhere, she slipped up and down, up to her room and down into the kitchen, with her hand on the banister rail. That was her path through life, her eyes empty milk-white balls. She had her meals with the family. She was treated well.

When my father was still at school, he, his mother and his aunt did not live in the farmer's house. They were housed in a shed next to it. If you live in a house, a proper house, you don't use the word 'housed', you say 'lived'. The shed had only one room with a tamped earth floor. Two tiny windows, neither bigger than a child's atlas. The beds were plank-beds and stood on high legs because it sometimes happened that after heavy rain the floor turned to mud. Oozing up from below. The feet of the beds were placed in bowls of water that needed to be topped up each night. To stop the bugs. How effective it was, I don't know. Bedbugs, so people said, can't swim and they can't jump like fleas either. But fleas can jump.

The richest man in Mariapfarr was a *Baumeister*, a master builder. His house was made of stone. A proper, large house, the ground floor built with rough stone blocks, the first and second floors with exposed timber beams and rendered walls, the window shutters dark red, with a large white diagonal stripe in the centre like those in a palace. There was a veranda on the south side. That house had more glass than all the other houses together. There was no cowshed built on to it, no barn. Even from far off it smelled of cement. That was one of the few things my father liked to tell us about: the smell of cement. A smell of the city. I like the smell of cement too. Freshly mixed cement, mmm! The builder's name was Brugger. And he owned a library.

I asked my father: 'How many books do you need to make it a library?'

He found the question very intelligent and praised me for it. Because he would praise me for it, I used to like asking him questions related to books. We were in 'our library' – in the library of the Convalescent Home for War-wounded. That is the second smell that I have loved since childhood: book dust. Cement and book dust – what more can you ask for?

'In here,' he said, 'there are 1,324 books. That can be considered a library.'

'And up to what number is it still not a library?' I asked.

'There needs to be at least one full bookcase,' he said. 'But one that goes from floor to ceiling and it has to be at least one metre wide. Then it counts.'

'And what kind of books do they have to be?'

'That is such a smart question,' he said.

Actually, it was not a question that I had just thought up off the top of my head. I had remembered what he had said one time: lining up any old rubbishy books on a shelf doesn't make a library out of them.

'When you look at a library,' he said as he limped past the shelves, running the fingernails of his right hand across the spines of the books, 'you know all there is to know about the person who owns them.'

The library of Baumeister Brugger from Mariapfarr in Lungau would not actually have qualified as one using my father's definition. The man owned – my father remembered this precisely and we knew precisely too, he had repeated it often enough – eighty-three titles. Only eighty-three titles. But the room in which the two shelves had been fixed to the wall, just two of them, had no other purpose. It was purely for reading. The only other things in the room were a leather armchair, a standing lamp and a small table and chair. Baumeister Brugger had intended to build up and establish a proper library one day, and when he designed his house, he had set aside a room for it. Later there had been so much else to sort out, he had kicked the library down the road, so to speak, until after retirement – this expression too came from my father, 'Kicking the library down the road,' he said, as if quoting the Baumeister, but full of contempt. Anyway, the family of Baumeister Brugger always referred to this room only as 'the library' or 'the study'. My father could remember every single book.

The Baumeister's son went to the same school as my father, an elementary school with only one class. My father was the brightest of all the children. The brightest by far, actually. He was so far ahead, he was almost a prodigy. According to family legend, he taught himself to read and write. When he was only five years old, two years before he started school. His mother used to borrow illustrated magazines regularly from the farmer's wife and read aloud from them to her blind sister. The boy sat beside them and listened. And asked his mother what reading was, how did what she was reading get on to paper and how did it go from there to her mouth. She showed him the letters and explained to him that there were only twenty-six of them and that the punctuation marks – the dash, the colon, the full stop, the question mark and so on – were not letters as such but were there to make the sentence understandable. The magazines were all old and after his mother had finished reading them, they were burned. One day the boy kept one of them for himself. Without asking. He hid it under his mattress. Even though the magazine was to be burned anyway, he had stolen it, and that gave him a guilty conscience. It was summer and a five-year-old had nothing to do except be a good boy, that meant to be quiet, not to be a bother, not to disturb the grown-ups. To stay out of the way. The boy was good at that. He tucked the magazine into his trousers, pulled his shirt over the top and went up into the woods. There he knew of a spot, in the shade, where ferns grew and there were mossy stones; there he sat himself down. Scraping with his foot, he cleared the ground around him to make a kind of writing tablet where he could trace characters with his index finger. He had learned to count a long time ago, only up to thirty it's true, but he had a good idea of what came next and had just not got around to counting any further. He did not know in what sequence the letters appeared in the alphabet. Just that there were twenty-six of them. Nor was he able to differentiate between capital letters and small letters. His mother had shown him only the capital letters. Most small letters looked nothing like the capital letters. Letter C was similar, and K and O; fairly similar were P, S, U and also V, and W and Z.

This confused him. That evening he laid the magazine on the table and confessed to his mother that he had stolen it. He was ready to take the punishment coming to him, if she would just solve for him the riddle of the small letters. He was expecting a cuff on the ears, which did not happen often. He did not know exactly the whys and wherefores of it, nor the why-nots. Sometimes for something that he himself considered a minor offence, such as when he put his shirt on the wrong way round. And then on the other hand, not for something serious, like smashing the sugar bowl. He never showed his pain. He never grimaced or made a sound when his mother beat him. It was as if she were beating a doll. My husband and I have a friend who is a psychiatrist and acts as an expert witness in legal cases. According to him, such shutting down by the victim can set off varying reactions: either even more violence, or a sense of horror at one's own violence. The victim, he said, surrenders his own body in the moment of pain, abandons it in a way, which is why the muscles are no longer able to react, preventing, too, any facial expression. On this occasion his mother laughed at him. Stealing was something different, something quite different. And she gave him a bit more help. He didn't need much. He caught on quickly.

He loved all the characters, both letters and numbers. Soon he was reading aloud to Aunt Vev. When his mother gave him a blue carpenter's pencil, a small knife for sharpening it and a bit of scrap paper, he sat quietly the whole day long, it was as if he wasn't there. When he finally started school, he could read and write better than those in the second class, better than those in the third class and better than many adults, quite a few of whom could not read at all.

My father was called Josef. There is a reason why I only mention this now. There are some names that carry a certain weight. The weight they carry can be as light as air or heavy. My sister Renate called her son Josef. After our father. And after our maternal grandfather. He had the same name. And then there was Uncle Josef. It was a name bestowed by destiny on our family, she said, and should be handed down. I know what she means by this. I would use a different word, not 'destiny'. But I don't want to think too much about which word, it's making me tired.

Renate lives in far-off Berlin, has lived there a long time. When I speak to her about our childhood, about our father, it seems to me that, with the many kilometres between his grave and her city, time has also stretched and become light. And with time, names have become light too. A memory like the smell of freshly mown grass or the floor of a pine forest on a summer afternoon.

We children never knew Grandfather Josef; he died young. There isn't even a photograph of him. But plenty of stories. He was apparently a good-looking man, envied by all the other men in the village. Above all because of his beautiful wife. They wanted to have what he had, that is, this beautiful woman, but no one wanted to change places with him, to be one of the poorest. I don't know if he was a good man. When his wife was pregnant with my future mother, he had to fight for the Kaiser down in Italy. He believed that my mother was not one of his. That someone else had sneaked in and lain with his wife while he was in the field. That's why he did not speak a single word to this child his whole life long. He did not believe the oaths sworn by his wife. And the others in the village did not believe her either.

Our people were known as the '*Bagage*', riff-raff. They were feared. They had their pride, and a shotgun with which my Uncle Lorenz, not yet eighteen at that point, and my Uncle Walter, still a boy, went out poaching, because otherwise they would have starved. The huntsmen used to send out a warning: stay out of the forest today, the Bagage kids are out shooting. Even at the age of sixteen Lorenz was someone about whom more tales were told than other men who had lived whole lifetimes. When his father was away at war, he had kept the mayor at bay with his shotgun, because the mayor was making unwanted advances towards his mother, the lovely Maria. Everyone in our family is convinced Lorenz would have fired if the mayor had not backed off.

The mayor himself used to regale people with the story everywhere. A different version, naturally.

My grandmother gave birth to seven children before she died at the age of thirty-two, three daughters: Kathe, Grete, my mother and Irma; and four sons: Heinrich, the oldest, Lorenz, Walter and the youngest, Josef, known as Sepp.

And then, the man with whom our future mother fell in love was of all things called Josef, too, a third one. Like her father, like her youngest brother, her favourite. That's what my sister Renate calls 'destiny'. In a way double destiny, because when our parents met, again there was a war, the second one this time – she was a nurse in a field hospital, he was a soldier whose leg had suffered frostbite and been amputated. And so, to carry on the name in the family, she had named her son Josef, Renate said. The fourth.

Baumeister Brugger was fond of Josef. He liked to see that his son was friends with him. He spoke his mind. Once he said: 'If it was possible to swap, I would.'

He said that to Josef's mother. He meant it as a compliment. Josef's mother smiled. She did not feel that she could contradict him.

The Baumeister took Josef under his wing. He had a word with the priest. Could something be done, so that the lad could go to a decent school. A school that was not just going through the motions, was what he meant. The grammar school, the

Gymnasium. This was a concept so far removed from Josef's mother that she did not even know the word. She always pronounced it wrong. 'Gunasion'. But she pronounced it incorrectly in such a confident way that no one made fun of her for it. Aunt Vev recalled that her confident mispronunciation made the school seem even grander than it actually was. Anyway, the priest said it would be possible, but only if Josef were later to join the clergy. The Baumeister agreed. The church gave him protection, though our dear Lord meant nothing to him.

When Josef visited the Baumeister's son, he planned it so the father would be at home. For his friend's father allowed him to sit in the library and read. He ordered his own child to leave Josef in peace. He told his wife the same.

To Josef he said: 'You can help yourself to any book on the shelf. I'm not going to tell you anything about it. Not about any of them. You need to find out for yourself what they have to say. Any questions?'

Josef shook his head.

He brought his school things with him. I reckon he was ten at the time. So he would already have had a notebook and not just a slate. He turned the notebook over and wrote down the names of the authors and the titles of the books, one below the other, at the back of the notebook. He wanted to read every book. In the sequence in which they stood on the two shelves in the Baumeister's library. But just reading was not enough for him. His whole life long reading was not enough. In this respect I am quite different from my father. Once I have read a book, I leave it lying around and at some point it seeps away into our home. The physical object does not interest me. After reading, its content is stored in my head. I prefer paperbacks. Because they are cheaper. For the price of a hardback you can afford three or four paperbacks. My father detested paperbacks. For him, his whole life, the physical object was just as important as its contents. That is an understatement. For him the book was sacred.

Before I introduced my husband to my father, I told him: 'He'll show you his library. He'll get you to pick up a book. The way you hold the book, how you leaf through it, how you take off the dust jacket, how you sniff at it, all these things will decide whether he will take to you or not.'

'What's the best way of doing it then?' asked my husband.

'I have no idea,' I said, 'I've never worked it out.'

My father did not want just to read a book; he wanted to possess it. He seldom borrowed books from libraries, from the town library, or the Chamber of Labour library, or the regional library or a distance loan from the National Library. He often visited these public institutions, selected here and there a book from the shelf, leafed through it, stroked it, sniffed it, read a few extracts, sometimes made a note of the author and title and later bought it.

In the library of Baumeister Brugger, he sat down at the little desk and started to copy out the first book. Into his notebook. Soon he was coming every afternoon after school. If her husband wasn't there, the farmer's wife took him into the study. She spoke in lowered tones. She brought him a glass of sweet woodruff lemonade. And said to her son he must not disturb Josef. When the notebook was full, he begged money from his mother or his aunt, or he stole notebooks out of the satchels of his schoolmates, tore out the pages that were already written on and buried them in the forest and then carried on copying out the book. Walter Scott, *Ivanhoe*, translated into German by Richard Zoozmann, 352 pages (it is lying beside me on my desk right now, I open it to the beginning). When his schoolmates reported that they had lost their notebooks, did not know where they could have gone, and the teacher scolded them for being such lazy rascals, and gave them detention or a beating with the cane, Josef sat on his bench and his face remained impassive, and if one of the pupils suggested that he had not lost his notebook at all, it had been stolen from his satchel, everyone in the class was under suspicion, except for one person: Josef.

Every day, he sat in Baumeister Brugger's study copying out.

In that pleasant district of merry England which is watered by the river Don, there extended in ancient times a large forest, covering the greater part of the beautiful hills and valleys which lie between Sheffield and the pleasant town of Doncaster. The remains of this extensive wood are still to be seen at the noble seats of Wentworth, of Warncliffe Park, and around Rotherham. Here haunted of yore the fabulous Dragon of Wantley; here were fought many of the most desperate battles during the Civil Wars of the Roses; and here also flourished in ancient times those bands of gallant outlaws, whose deeds have been rendered so popular in English song. Such being our chief scene …

The Baumeister's son was tugging at him. Josef had come over to his place to play and now all he did was sit in the study. Josef looked at him, looked him directly in the eyes and said: 'Do you want me to tell your father that you're disturbing me?'

'What are you actually doing in the study?' asked the lad.

'Something important,' said Josef.

'Does Papa know what you are doing?'

'Yes.'

'Are you going to tell me what you're doing?'

'No.'

'Why not?'

'It's a secret.'

'What's it to do with?'

'I'm not allowed to say.'

'Something to do with politics?'

'I'm not allowed to say.'

'Well, what if I ask my father, what then?'

'Then he'll say that it's none of your business.'

'But he's my father, not yours.'

'Your father and I have a secret mission to fulfil. Something very important.'

'I don't believe you.'

'I don't care if you believe me or you don't believe me.'

'Why can't I join in?'

'Because you're too stupid.'

'I am not stupid.'

'That's what all stupid people think.'

'I'm better than you are.'

'And what use is that to you?'

I already mentioned that my father did not talk much about himself, and he was even less willing to speak of his time as a child. But he used to talk about this conversation. Often. On each occasion as if he was telling us about it for the first time. And always slightly differently. And always with an undertone of venom. We knew what had become of Baumeister Brugger's son. When the Nazis came to power in Austria, he was one of the first to join the Hitler Youth. He rose through the ranks quickly and before he turned twenty he'd moved to Salzburg, to the city, and become a member of the SS. He is supposed to have been one of the organisers of the book burning there. From the manner in which my father talked about him, I inferred that the Baumeister's son had only done all this to show his childhood friend, Josef, that he too had it up top. He made it through the war unscathed; my father lost many of his hopes and half a leg. One–nil to the Baumeister's son.

At some point, the Baumeister realised what Josef was doing in the study. That he was not just reading. By this time ten notebooks had been filled. In tiny, neat handwriting. Almost a third of *Ivanhoe*. Baumeister Brugger was moved. To the depths of his heart. That books could mean so much to a ten-year-old boy! 'Well, do you want to copy out my whole library?' he exclaimed. He was so moved that tears ran down his cheeks. His cheeks had a dusting of fine cement because he had come direct from a building site – of course, he always came from a building site – and the tears left visible traces on both sides of his nose, round the corners of his mouth and over his double chin into his shirt collar where they disappeared. His wife got a fright and thought something must have happened, a burn from a chemical or something like that. She asked what had happened. 'The most amazing thing that you or I have ever experienced,' said her husband, and told her the story, 'and we'll never experience something so amazing ever again as long as we live.' His wife was not moved, she found it repulsive. To her it was as if the boy were gobbling up the book. First the book and then, what next? And in the end the Baumeister found it repulsive too. He made a gift of *Ivanhoe* to Josef (the same copy that is lying beside me on the desk). And he stopped inviting him into the library in his house. He also didn't want his son to go around with him any more.

'Josef has nothing in common with you. I really don't know who he does have something in common with.'

This skinny, pale boy – he could read nothing in his face, nor could his wife, nor could his son, no one could, nor would ever be able to – seemed alien to him. He had promised the priest that he would put something towards Josef's education. He never did. The Baumeister of Mariapfarr in Lungau did not keep his word.

The priest took care of Josef. He had smiled in amusement about the book copying. It was exactly what the monks of the Middle Ages had done all day long, and had they not done that, he said, things would have been very different today. He enrolled Josef at the Gymnasium in Salzburg. And organised a place for him at a Catholic boarding house for boys.

Josef was a good student, not necessarily always top of the class, but never with less than a 'satisfactory' in his school report, and that would only have been for the physical education class, which no one cared about anyway. He travelled home at Christmas and Easter and in the summer holidays. He often volunteered for cleaning duties at the boarding house, so that he could stay a bit longer and would not have to go straight home. He liked being in the boarding house. There was a lovely feeling of solitude when he went to bed in the dormitory in the evenings together with the fifty other boys, wrapped his pillow around his head, breathing in the smell of beeswax and moth powder, and drifted into a dreamworld until he fell asleep and his real dreams came to him.

Six months before sitting the *Matura*, his school-leaving-certificate exam, he was called up for war service. As far as I know, he was posted soon afterwards to Russia, it was impossible to extract further details from him. They went to an extremely cold region. One day the young soldiers ran across a field with the temperature at -30°C, and the wind blew in their faces so that it felt like -40°C or even colder, and then they reached a forest, where it was only -15°C. There they were sheltered from the wind, it felt like a cosy sitting room. The soldiers lay down, rested their heads on the tree roots, hands tucked under the left or right cheek because they were so tired and longed so much for their beds at home and they fell asleep, and many of them got frostbite, some of them lost just a hand or an arm. Our father his right leg. 'They died or almost died, as heroes or idiots' – that's what I heard our Uncle Lorenz say more than once.

Our father was brought to the field hospital, where his lower leg was amputated and in the field hospital he met Grete Moosbrugger. She became our mother.

We called her *Mutti*, not Mama. Our father wanted it that way. Because he thought it sounded modern. Modern our mother was not. She came from the remotest backwoods, her brothers were a wild bunch. When their parents died, the oldest, Uncle Heinrich, was just seventeen or eighteen. The children had to fend for themselves. No one helped them. They didn't have faith in the Church nor in Hitler. Well, Aunt Irma did have faith in Hitler. For her, he was modern. Uncle Lorenz said she shouldn't put her hopes in him. She never had anyway, she said after the war. Our father was convinced that people living in such circumstances were better somehow, deep down. Like him. He also came from a sort of down-and-out family. He used to quote Rilke: 'For poverty is a great glow from within.' But the way he quoted it, it sounded as if he was referring to other people, not to us, as if he were looking at the poor, but was himself not one of them, as if he just wanted to highlight the glow. As if he were able to see things in an objective, fair-minded way. I think my father believed that those who come from the absolute depths, from the most miserable hovel in the countryside, have an easier time of it in the city. They have nothing that they have to leave behind. They feel no longing for fields, meadows and livestock. They come into the city and quickly settle down. As long as they learn. First and foremost, the language of the city and the language of the new age.

All the children around us called their parents Mama and Papa. Our mother used to chide her husband softly: 'If they really want to call me Mama, just let them.' She herself had never spoken to her own father. Because he had never spoken to her. We used to call her Mama, until our father came through the door, and then we'd call her Mutti. And soon, we just said Mutti. Mutti and Vati. When other children came to visit us, I avoided calling my parents anything, and when I was at school and was telling some anecdote about life at home, I said Mama and Papa. Only later, when we lived in the city, and our mother was no longer alive, and I heard other children also saying Mutti and Vati, did I fall into line. And in the end, I even called our stepmother Mutti.

When they met, the war was over for him. He was not quite convinced though. Had kept on looking at the blue-red stump below his knee. As if something could be done with it. As if someone might still send him back to the front. With one leg, you can still shoot, he used to say, you just can't run away. Our future mother was not quite convinced either. As a nurse in the field hospital, she had seen men who were held together only by their uniform. How could anyone make sense of the orders? It was as if the two of them were observing the world from outside. As if they found themselves embroiled in it by chance. In this mess. This 'shambles of a war'. A world in which anything seemed possible. Where even a wounded man could be sent back to the front.

It might normally be expected that he, as the man, would be the one to make a promise about the future to her, but he did not. In the end, it was left to her, Grete. For she could not bear the thought that this wounded man would leave before he had proposed to her. She had the idea that there were no longer enough men to go around, so that soon there would be no one left for her. What she secretly hoped was that she would not be left on the shelf. Everything else was secondary. She did not think of herself as beautiful. He, on the other hand, was good looking and would look even better as soon as he was given enough to eat and the sun had banished the pallor from his face. He had looked at her so affectionately when she had taken leave of him for the night. In the field hospital, the simplest 'goodnight' was a leave-taking, just in case. He was now practising walking with crutches and she helped him, but he hadn't really got the hang of it yet. Which she was pleased about, as he would still need her for quite a long time. She often had to catch hold of him, this light man, who unquestionably weighed less than her. She was plump, she didn't know if he liked that. An *Ingenieur* came and fitted him for a prosthesis. He measured his right foot for the left orthopaedic shoe, it was to be fixed after that to the prosthesis, glued on. Should she point out to the man that the prosthetic foot really needed to be made the other way round, so Josef didn't end up with two right feet? Grete suspected that the prosthetist was not really a qualified specialist, that's why he gave himself the title Ingenieur.

Now Josef won't need me any more. That was her worry. Once when I spoke to my sister Renate about it, she said: 'Maybe she imagined herself to be someone who is needed rather than loved?'

I said: 'She was shy. Though when it really mattered, she wasn't shy. But *he* was, especially then.'

She made the proposal of marriage. So forcefully, that right there and then – that is, standing there with his fitted prosthesis – he said, 'Yes.'

She knew absolutely nothing about him. And when everything was finally settled, she stood in front of him like a shy schoolgirl again. And he stood there in a white shirt and trousers that were two sizes too big for him, then he sat down on a hospital chair by the wall. Everything he had was donated, he possessed nothing. Nothing at all. I can hardly imagine someone having absolutely nothing, nothing at all. I hear people say: 'We were facing ruin.' And then it turns out that their shoes belonged to them, their socks, and their umbrella and the cap on their head too. In my father's case, at that time my father-to-be, nothing meant: nothing. One did not even own the dirt beneath one's fingernails, it had been scratched from other people's window frames. Because he was so slight, one could have brought him some school-boy's clothes to put on. Grete had applied a little lipstick and put waves in her hair in order to bring a sense of urgency and occasion to her proposal. He took her hand, rough from much plunging in water, pulled it to his heart and repeated: 'Yes.'

His hair almost reached his shoulders, it badly needed cutting, he looked like a girl. He drew her head towards him and kissed her awkwardly on the mouth. Their first kiss. Can you believe it? My mother always cut my father's hair until she was no longer capable of it. Not ours, just his.

Grete told her sisters first, Katharina and Irma, and could they pass on the news to their brothers, to Walter, Heinrich and Sepp. Lorenz was still away at the war. Grete told them in her letter of the beautiful conversations that she had had with this man. Heinrich had commented: 'So apart from thinking, he can't do much.'

Our father had lied to our mother. He had told her he had no one. Not only nothing, but on top of that no one. His parents had died when he was a child, he said. No relatives. And so on and so forth. He had painted an alternative picture of his origins for her. Had actually created his own portrait. Not rich people, of course, but also not so miserably poor.

It was the war that had taken everything from him, before that he had done all right. In his stories he was not from Lungau, but from the city of Salzburg. He was a city boy. He told her his stories with such fervour that she did not believe him. But that didn't matter. In the meantime, everyone accepted that the world had changed. The latest news reports from the collapsing empire accepted that the world had changed.

'I come from the furthest backwoods,' Grete had said. And that was the truth. 'My parents are long dead.' That was the truth too. 'We were the poorest of the poor.' This too was true and was probably still true. Although it was impossible to know everything that had been going on in the meantime in the backwoods. Fairy-tale endings were possible. Marvels. But then again probably not.

In the chaos at the end of the war, no one noticed if a cripple went missing. Actually, it was a plus if one went missing. Without signing out, they made their escape from the field hospital. Grete helped herself to two crutches for him and a coat belonging to one of the doctors. Two were hanging in the cloakroom, a good one and a better one. She took the better one. She took him to the backwoods. To her family. To the small rundown family home with the empty cowshed and the empty barn. Her brother Lorenz was still in Russia. What exactly he was up to, no one knew. Nor even if he was still alive. No letters had been delivered from there for some time. Katharina, my future Aunt Kathe, ruled the roost in the small house on the mountainside, the last house before the mountain, where a stream flowed by, into which a concrete basin had been sunk, you could get into it on hot days, the water up to your chest. Kathe said they needed to be prepared for the fact that Lorenz might never return from Russia.

When Grete introduced Josef to her, Kathe said: 'If you like, I'll act as priest and marry you both.'

Josef laughed because he thought she was making a joke, a friendly, welcoming joke. It was not a joke. Priests were an abomination to my Aunt Kathe her whole life long. Once, when she was still a child and Grete was a very small child, still in her pram, the priest had come with a lad and tools and taken down the crucifix on the outside of their house, because supposedly little Grete had been fathered by another man. For that Kathe had never forgiven the priest-hood in general.

Also in the house up in the forest, at the foot of the rock face, lived the younger siblings – Walter, Sepp and Irma. Heinrich, the eldest, had moved out; he was dealing in cattle and goats and in wild game and was successful and had taken a lease on a farm of his own. He was no longer to be seen up in the forest. He was scared of his siblings, he could not make them out, with their stubborn pride. He was embarrassed if one of his customers enquired whether he was related to that lot. He would grunt something unintelligible. He didn't want to deny it outright, superstitious as he was.

Everyone liked Grete's frail husband. Especially Sepp. For a start because they shared the same name. Vati taught him to play chess. They cobbled together a chessboard. A piece of cardboard on which they marked out the squares in ink. They fashioned the chess pieces out of dough. They put them in the stovepipe and baked kings, queens, knights, castles and pawns. From the start Sepp wanted to play for money. The smallest amounts, but money. My father told me once when he was trying to teach chess to me too, that Uncle Sepp had picked it up straight away and was very quickly a match for him. It was clear there was an implied reproach, namely that I had not picked it up straight away. From that moment on, I lost interest in chess, because I could never be as good as my Uncle Sepp. Uncle Lorenz could play chess even better – I am getting ahead of myself here. And with that I have also let slip that he did come back home from Russia in the end.

So now they all lived together in Grete's family home. What did they survive on? My Aunt Kathe used to answer this question with: 'No one has the slightest idea.' The smallholding was a thing of the past. No cow, no goats, only a few hens and a rooster. I do know a little bit: my father helped the people in the village in their dealings with bureaucracy. They came to see him. They considered him to be someone special. Firstly, because he was an outsider, secondly, he was not a complete foreigner but an Austrian like them, just not a local man, and above all, not a Frenchman from the occupying forces, but someone who was able to deal with the French in an easy manner to everyone's benefit, and in addition, was able to speak and understand their language even if at a basic level. That meant a lot. People said: finally the Bagage have someone that will look out for them. In their eyes, that could only be someone from a higher class of society or at least a slightly higher one. It was not difficult to be a step up from the Bagage, they were at the bottom of the pile. From their first impressions of the new arrival, they inferred he would be a good influence. A city lad of course. Why had he chosen Grete from the Bagage? It was a mystery. I don't know when my father told our mother the truth about his origins. Almost certainly when once again nothing mattered any more.

My father also helped his brother-in-law Heinrich, who, it's true, did not want to have anything more to do with his siblings, but in the end did come to accept Grete's husband. Because he was useful. When Heinrich changed his leasehold into a freehold, Vati handled all the negotiations with the owner and with the bank. He did not do it for free. He did not even offer a family discount. Sepp advised him: 'Every last penny!' This increased Heinrich's respect for our father.

Our mother and father were very close to each other in these early days. Both Aunt Kathe and Aunt Irma mentioned this. With Irma, I had the impression she was jealous. She was a very beautiful woman, had inherited her mother's beauty. She had always believed that she could have any man she wanted and could bide her time. And because she was so convinced of this, each man fell short. And so for a long time, she did not have one.

In the small house at the foot of the mountain, they now all lived together not knowing how they survived but surviving somehow. What was previously the parental bedroom belonged to Vati and Mutti. My mother told me later that the pillow had still smelled of her parents. They had been dead and buried a long time by then. Her father's pillow had smelled of campfires, of adventure, a smell which scared her a bit. Because she'd been scared of her father. Because his whole life long he had acted as if she didn't exist. Her mother's pillow smelled of carnations. She didn't know why, where could the scent of carnations have come from? She could not remember that there had ever been a carnation in the house. 'Perhaps it was from one of Grandmother's perfumes,' I said. 'No,' said Mutti, 'she had no need of perfume.'

In the summer Sepp, the youngest, slept outside on the veranda, one blanket on the ground, one over his body and head, done. Oh, yes, I forgot something: they had a dog. He belonged to Sepp and slept beside him. Sepp looked like his father, the people in the village said, and Irma was like her mother. Sometimes when you saw them walking along, you could almost believe that their parents had risen from their graves. Some in the village had a guilty conscience because they'd been unpleasant and unjust to the parents when they were still alive – or to be blunt, malicious and mean – and so they would leave a gift at the house from time to time. It would simply appear on the doorstep. Sepp said he'd been woken up early in the morning more than once by the dog growling, but by then the friendly spirits had always disappeared. Once there was even a banana in the gift basket. Sepp had polished that off, still half asleep. He hadn't had a guilty conscience, still half asleep he'd thought he was dreaming and the banana had tasted dreamy too. Our father had a different version: Sepp had shared the banana with him. They had agreed to keep silent and had swirled the chewed banana pulp around in their mouths as long as possible.

Katharina was worried about Walter. He was the wildest one. He didn't listen to her. And he didn't listen to his brother-in-law, Josef, either. Our father was by this time the head of the household, but he could not cope with Walter. Walter was already in his mid-thirties, roamed around the whole valley as a general farmhand, was still single and always fired up. That is, he was always chasing after women, after every single one; more than once someone threatened to put a bullet through his head. 'I can't stand it any more!' That was his stock phrase.

My father took him to one side, he thought he knew the solution.

'You belong in a city,' he said to him. 'If someone says he can't stand it, he belongs in a city. And you say that three times a day.'

'So I should go to Bregenz?' asked Walter. 'Why would it be any better there?'

'Not Bregenz,' said my father. 'You're such a country bumpkin! Do you think there's only one city? And it's a tiny place like your Bregenz?'

'Well, which city should I go to then?'

'To Vienna, for example.'

'Definitely not Vienna, definitely not to those morons, definitely not.'

'Well, Berlin then.'

'And who's going to pay my expenses for that?'

'I'll give you the money.'

'Where will you get it from?'

My father wanted to get rid of him, it's true, and Walter knew that, but did not hold it against him. Josef, the husband of his sister Grete, was after all the only person in the world to believe that he was capable of making his way in the big city of Berlin. For that he would have happily blessed his brother-in-law. If he had believed in blessings. He didn't. One day he set off. But he only got as far as Bregenz before turning back.

When my sister was born, Vati wanted her to be named after her mother: Margarethe. Family lore has it that our father pushed our heavily pregnant mother to the maternity hospital on a sled, stumbling and staggering on his peg leg into the next village.

Eighteen months later, I arrived. I don't remember the time in the small house in the forest in the shadow of the mountain. My father was offered the post of manager in the Convalescent Home for War-wounded on the Tschengla Plateau. It was there, in that paradise, that I first became aware that I was an individual – someone who could say 'I'.

I am tired. I close my laptop, stretch, it is only early afternoon. It is not the writing that makes me tired, nor is it the remembering. I want to be tired. I use tiredness as a professional tool. I need to get closer to the dreams, not quite asleep but no longer totally awake, remembering comes more easily this way, that's my experience, I want to make use of this phenomenon. I am conjuring. What a lovely expression! I conjure up the sound of our mother coming up the stairs, taking off her dress and giving her skin a scratch. I used to love hearing that, then I knew: now she's putting on her fresh white nightshirt, which has been carefully pressed, and before she goes into the main bedroom, she'll cuddle up with us girls for a quarter of an hour. Did we even know the phrase 'cuddle up'? I don't think so. That is a city turn of phrase. She came out of the washhouse, where there was a stone tub and a wide washbasin hooked on to the wall and our washing things lay on a porcelain shelf and our facecloths and hand towels hung on enamel hooks. My whole life long I have been on the lookout for this special soap scent. Sometimes, where it is least expected, it wafts past. My son Lorenz, the painter, says if smells could be described accurately, they could be ordered on the internet. That made us laugh. Lorenz calls me up and says: 'If you need anything, Mama, give me a shout.' He means for my research. If he can help me at all, he means. I say: I am trying to rely on my memory, that has to suffice. If I were to find this soap in a drugstore, I'd buy a multipack, one hundred bars, I would put on a common-sense face, a bit stressed-looking, and make out that I had to buy in bulk for a school boarding house …

Through daydreams I drift back in time, I imagine the summer meadow, wrap my head in my pillow, which the guests from Inner Austria called a *Polster* – 'Could I have a second *Polster* please?' I dream myself up to the Tschengla Plateau, 1,220 metres above sea level, back to the year 1955, when I was eight. The meadow is on a steep slope, in some places so steep that when I bend forward, I can lean against the ground with my arm bent. From far off, the meadow looks deep blue, as if a scribe up above had emptied out his ink pot over it, when you look more closely, they turn out to be finger-sized flowers with goblet-shaped heads. Blue gentians. And peeping out cheekily from among them, small spring gentians. The inky blue is so restful for the eyes. I lie down in the meadow, the grass rises above my forehead, I dig my heels into the ground so that I can get a grip and don't slip. I turn on to my stomach, cling to the grass. There are so many tiny things to be seen. An earwig. You have to be careful of them. Deep under the green lies the brown and decaying and the cool and damp. There are beetles, some I know: the stag beetle, you seldom see those; the rose chafer that has a gold-green metallic sheen; the May bug, the hairy one that's destructive and that we're supposed to catch – for one kilo you get one schilling – but that usually sits too high up in the trees munching away; and then the ladybird with seven black spots, I place one on my hand and stretch my finger up into the air and it crawls to the top and flies off. I know the butterflies too: the cabbage white, the brimstone, the admiral, the peacock butterfly, the small blue one whose name escapes me right now. My sister Gretel and I are holding fir cones in our hands, dry ones that have already sprung open, we stick them full of gentians, carefully so that the delicate blue sides of the goblet don't tear. Back at home, we put them in water, they suck it all up, the scales close up and the flowers stay fresh for a long time. We give them as a present to our Mutti. No special reason. Just because she is our

Mutti. She says, oh, how lovely, but somehow up in the meadow they're even more beautiful. Don't think that I don't like your present, she says, but imagine if a hundred children did the same thing, the meadow would be bare. I am hurt, offended, and think that I can never be happy again and say, well, that's the last time, never again, ever, and I tell her that I reckon there are at least millions or even twice that many flowers growing in the meadow, and would she rather they just withered, for that's what happens, within just a week or so they'll have withered in the middle of the meadow. My sister looks down at her bare feet. Yes, we are barefoot. In the spring we feel our way cautiously and painfully over the sharp stones, but then when our skin has toughened up, at the latest by June, we run over sticks and stones as if we were wearing shoes or as if there was no such thing as shoes. They lie all summer long in the space under the stairs, spiders' webs all over them. Even on Sundays we go barefoot, brown feet, only the spaces between our toes still white. Your feet, shoulders and the tip of your nose get the most suntanned, my father explained to me. Because the sun's rays shine down directly on them. Because we walk upright, unlike the apes. I especially like it when it has rained in the night, then we bound straight out in the morning and leap into the puddles looking for a place where it's muddy and I can move my feet about in it, so that the mud squelches up through my toes – it is warm and soft, we know that it's clean and not disgusting, like stepping barefoot into a fresh cowpat, which is the same sort of feeling. Afterwards our feet are covered with grey mud, we sit on the edge of the veranda and stretch them out in the sun until they dry off and the mud is crumbling away and our skin is itching a bit. At lunchtime the rule is wash your hands but not wash your feet.

I daydream and take delight in the forget-me-not in the meadow, the speedwell, the cuckoo flower, the arnica. The moss that grows on the windward side of the tree trunks and makes the bark look crusty, in every shade from pure yellow to grey. The three tall birch trees that grow in their circular bed in front of the Convalescent Home for War-wounded, ringed by knee-high stones. The spiral wooden columns that support the elegant little tiled porch roof over the entrance to the Home.

Thirty years later, I drove with my husband and small children up to the Tschengla in our old VW bus, which was red and orange. For the first time since everything happened. The meadow looked more sparse, but was still colourful, I wanted to dig out a piece with a spade and take it back down to our house in the valley and plant it in our garden. I said to my husband it was not as beautiful as before, not so lush, not so colourful. He said he had never before seen such a beautiful, such a colourful, such a lush meadow. We lay down in the grass, the children lay still, arms and legs stretched out, but we two kept sliding downwards, that's how steep the meadow is. I showed my husband how to dig his heels into the ground. We lay there like that and I told him stories. Sometimes Gretel and I had taken a shortcut and left the path and gone home across the meadow, but it took us longer, we fell a lot and slid downhill. It was like mountain climbing, said my husband. We wove daisy chains for our hair, and for our little brother, Richard, who looked so cute, always a quiff on top of his head, like a cream-horn pastry. I always used to worry about him, I continued, at any rate while he was still in the pram. Gretel and I plucked the flower petals from a daisy and sang: he loves me, he loves me not, he loves me … We didn't know who we were talking about, who it was that loved us or didn't love us, we thought the song was simply a song and that the words of a song didn't mean anything, they were just there for singing, often we sang la-la-la.

But I also have to mention the worms and how I cut them into two or more pieces with scissors and how I explained to my sister Gretel, who found this disgusting, that it didn't harm the worm, that he would continue having a happy life, and now there were three of them and he was not all alone any more, if he could talk, he would be thanking me. I bet my schoolfriend, Emil, that I would swallow a worm before his very eyes, and that's what I did.

But then in the night, the worm grew and it soon felt like the tapeworm in the picture in the children's encyclopaedia. I woke my parents up whimpering. Our father took me by the hand, in the middle of the night, and we left the Home, him in his pyjamas, me in my nightdress, and he led me past the birches over to the shed which was not used for anything and where he had set up a *Laboratorium*. I think that '*Laboratorium*' was the first foreign word that I ever heard in my life. Our father would have liked to become a chemist. At that time, he was going to evening school. Two days a week he was not up on the mountain with us but down in the town where he had rented a tiny room. He wanted to pick up his studies for the Matura certificate again and then continue studying. And move into the city with his family. Any city. He led me into the shed, switched on the light and said I was to sit on the stool, he was going to show me something. He disappeared and came straight back with an earthworm between his index finger and thumb. He laid the worm in a saucer, opened one of the bottles that stood on the table against the wall and sprinkled a few drops onto the worm. It wriggled around, foamed up and turned white. And was dead. That's what happens in your stomach, said my father. That was hydrochloric acid. Your stomach contains hydrochloric acid too. And if it were not there, we would starve. And now I had to go back to bed and stop fantasising that there was a worm in my stomach and that it was growing in there, what a load of nonsense.

We had a cook and a maid. And if I may continue to show off, we also had a nanny. The nanny was our Aunt Irma, my mother's younger sister, at that time still unmarried but being courted assiduously by her soon-to-be husband, a blind colossus. The maid was called Lotte. She spoke to everyone in her broad dialect, our father was the only one she spoke to differently. Not because she thought that he would not understand her, coming as he did from Salzburg; she spoke also to the German guests in dialect, and when someone asked her what she had said, she explained it a different way but still in broad dialect, without softening it at all, grimacing as she did so and pronouncing more distinctly what had not been understood, but it was still incomprehensible. She spoke formal high German to our father, because she saw him as being a cut above. A man with a future. A proper future. His background was irrelevant. And because she liked him. This was the only way she dared to show him her feelings. And then one evening, as the sinking sun threw a trail of red across the summit of the Mondspitze and we were all sitting on the veranda – except for our father, he was in the library – I listened as Lotte told us about the eagle that circled over this mountain every evening. You'll see it any second now! And we saw it. The cook had told her, said Lotte, that the bird took babies from their cradle when they were asleep, and brought them up with its own young, up in the eagle's eyrie in the middle of the rock face, pushed half-dead mice into their mouths, heaped soft down over them on cold nights, and then when the eaglets were big enough, they would slaughter the babies and polish them off for their evening meal. They would rip open their bellies and pick out the red meat. Eaten alive. Our brother had just been born and soon he was put out on the sun terrace in the bassinet. The net on the bassinet looked flimsy, fluttered in the wind – you could hardly see our Richard's little head, and I couldn't help imagining the eagle ripping Richard out of his cradle with its claws and clutching him like prey, then flying with him up to the Mondspitze and dropping him in its nest. I had an image of Richard bleeding from the eagle's claws, his little arms all scratched, his romper suit in shreds, soon he would be lying naked in the eagle's nest and the eaglets would play with his little white body. I perched on a stool in front of his cradle to watch over him and panicked that if it happened, I would be to blame because I was the one who was supposed to be looking after him. There was no way out, the eagle was going to swoop down on him. And of course I had not even taken account of the female eagle! I think I wept the whole night long – did no one comfort me? Father probably said to our mother, just let her cry, it strengthens the lungs, we don't want to be spoiling her.

'Your father,' said my stepmother, 'stashed away a third of the books from the Convalescent Home for War-wounded library.'

'Swiped them.' It was a statement, not a question. 'You mean, he swiped them. That's what you really mean.'

'Stole,' she said. 'I said "stashed away" so it didn't sound so brutal. But it doesn't really matter anyway. In front of a court it's immaterial whether a person swipes, or steals, or stashes away, it comes to the same thing. And when he realised his plan wasn't working, and that he was about to get caught, he mixed some poison in his clever laboratory and drank it and nearly died from it. Did you know that?'

'Yes, I knew that – no, I didn't know that.'

'Gretel knew about it, she should have told you. Why didn't she tell you? I have a pretty good idea why she didn't tell you. You should give Gretel a lot of credit for that …'

'What plan?' I interrupted her.

'Plan, plan!' she exclaimed loudly and bent over the table and grabbed the cigarette box that she had deliberately pushed out of reach because she'd been trying to stop smoking for at least the last sixty years, and plucked one out and lit it with the lighter. 'What plan! What sort of plan do you think? He just liked the idea of being a man who had his own library. He wanted to have the books. That was a fine collection.'

'And how would you know that?' I said. 'You never went up to the Tschengla. You never saw the library, you have no idea!'

'He told me about the library, he said it was an outstanding collection. Shouldn't I believe him? His plan was to acquire the library for himself. Slowly, slowly, piece by piece. So that in the end everyone would be convinced that it belonged to him, to Josef.'

'That's your version,' I said.

'Do you have a different one?'

I didn't.

Of course, I knew that our father could be unscrupulous in his addiction to books. Lacking any social conscience. Long after we had moved away from the Tschengla, when our mother was no longer alive and he had remarried and we were all living on top of one another in a cramped apartment in Bregenz, and when he was working for the Department of Finance and in his spare time finessing tax returns for cash in hand, the money he made was spent exclusively on books. This is how he justified to himself his disloyalty to his employer – the important thing is not how one gets one's income but what one spends it on. And when our stepmother quarrelled with him, quarrelled with good reason because she thought that her children needed new shoes in winter, he called me over and asked if I was happy with my old shoes, and I said, yes, I am. Because I wanted to help him out. Although my shoes had holes and I ran around with wet feet. He had no guilt about that. Not any more. At some point he had stopped feeling guilt. Towards whom, anyway? Towards whoever had taken his wife away from him? Towards whoever made it so that a man freezes when he has wet feet? What are wet feet compared with an amputated leg? Books are too cheap, he used to say. He despised paperbacks. Such shoddy editions were like someone worming themselves insidiously into another person's head. He never treated himself to anything. Holidays, never. New clothes, only with reluctance. Which is why our stepmother never checked with him first, she simply laid the new things in the closet. No car. He did not even permit himself an umbrella, he would take one from the office if someone had left one behind.

'He no longer knew which way to turn at that point,' said my stepmother and sighed into her cloud of smoke, and I didn't know how I was supposed to interpret this sigh: as sympathetic or disparaging? 'He'd have been thrown out. Dismissed. Without notice. Probably charged. No, definitely. Germans don't mess around. You would've had to move out. Theft. And to cap it all, theft of something that was meant for the poorest of the poor, for the war-wounded. Taking from them, that would not have gone down well in any court. He'd have been ruined. You would all have been ruined. You would've all been finished.'

'Not one of the guests,' I said, and I noticed my throat tightening, 'not one ever took out a single book, not one. Not a single one ever entered the library. Our father was the only one who took any interest in the books! Without him they would all have mouldered away. They would have had to be thrown out or flogged off in a flea market. He built the bookcases, he made them himself and he dusted them regularly. I know he did because I often used to help him. I know he did!'

'Simmer down!' said my stepmother and lit up again.

How did the Convalescent Home for War-wounded up on the Tschengla, a long way from anywhere, high up in the mountains, where people did not even subscribe to a newspaper, come by such a valuable library? For it was indeed valuable. Most of the books bound in leather. Or half leather. Magnificent editions of the works of Goethe and Schiller and Lessing and so on, the classics. But also scientific works, books of philosophy; ten volumes of Immanuel Kant, for example, bound in umber leather, with gilt edges. I have no real memory of the books mentioned above, I was a child and knew very little about them. In one of the school notebooks that my father kept his whole life – where he made haphazard notes for himself about books – he had listed the titles and authors in the library in his tiny handwriting. Of his favourite books, that is. I have a few of those notebooks in my possession. We siblings shared them out between us after his death. I can't see anything personal in them, no diary entries.

He often took me with him into the room at the end of the house, probably intended as a storeroom, where there were only two tiny little windows high up near the ceiling, he had to climb up a small wooden ladder to open them. Because the roof of the house had a wide overhang – firewood was piled up against the wall out of the rain – hardly any light penetrated inside. A fir tree growing at the front also robbed us of light, but smelled very nice. All I could see was its trunk, with sap spilling out in several places. All along the ceiling above the shelves, my father had fitted small lights, directed onto the books. He'd made the ladder himself as well. In the middle of the room stood a table, just sixty by sixty centimetres, two chairs in front of it, kitchen chairs, painted white, bits of paint flaking off. That was all. No carpet, just a wooden floor. An electric fire with glowing red bars for heating in winter. The walls from top to bottom full of books.

'Come with me, Monika,' he would say every now and then. I remember it as always raining when I was in the library with him, in there the world was left behind. He switched the light on, a magical sheen lay on the spines of the books. 'Come on, let's have a browse!' he said.

'Can you show me the most beautiful one?' I asked – or I didn't ask. If we were both in that same room now, I would ask this question – or not.

He used to climb up the ladder and run his fingernail across the spines of the books, a soft, click-click-click could be heard, the room pervaded by a murky silence, the books absorbing every outside noise.

'Here … this one …' he would say and pull out a book – the one now lying beside my laptop, on top of *Ivanhoe* – still on the ladder he would open up the book, reddish-brown leather, the title with its old German spelling and the name of the author in gold lettering: *The Expression of the Emotions in Man and Animals* by Charles Darwin. He would hand the book down to me. 'Put it on the table, we'll have a look at it together.'

I would put on a serious face, like on Sundays at communion in church, take the book and hold it in my hands until my father had climbed down from the ladder; hard leather, not as soft and supple as *Ivanhoe*. The book is richly illustrated, steel engravings, one whole page just of faces of apes, in one the lips pushed way forwards, as if the fellow were saying: please, be careful. And then the prominent eyebrows drawn up into his forehead as if to say: well, that was a mean thing to do! Then an angry, dangerous set of teeth: don't come too close! On another page, comparisons with humans – sad face, happy face, malice, fright, vengefulness, tenderness, reverence. I remember how proud my father was because I was so enthralled and so enthusiastic. As if he had written the book himself. Or even as if he himself had invented apes and humans.

How did these books come to be in the Convalescent Home for War-wounded?

A man from Swabia in south-western Germany had left them to the Home in his will. A professor from Tübingen. An academic in the humanities. The word for his profession in German is *Geisteswissenschaftler*, literally, a scientist of the spirit. I first heard this word used by my father. I found it a bit creepy; probably because of the 'spirit' part I imagined the man as a kind of ghost. The professor had a son who had also been in the war, and had lost half a leg like our father plus an arm as well and three-quarters of his mind. He was an only child. He had been a budding artist. A painter. Had also played the violin. He could have become anything: a painter, musician, poet. He had written poems, he had wanted to write like Hölderlin. As a student he had taken no interest in politics, just in beauty. He'd been called up close to the end of the war. And was shot and severely injured almost straight away and lay in the dirt and one army vehicle ran over his leg and another ran over his arm. When he came back, he couldn't do anything any more, could no longer play the violin, no longer paint, no longer write poetry, he could not even read properly any more, because he couldn't remember a sentence after reading it on the page. I don't know much about it. The young man's mother lapsed into depression, his father thought the mountains would do him good. So they sent him to us, to the Convalescent Home for War-wounded on the Tschengla. He stayed for a year. That had not actually been the plan. No one was actually supposed to stay that long. The normal session lasted at most one month. It was not called 'leave' or 'holiday', we called it 'session'. The young man was an exception. Only because my father did not put him down in the register. He simply took him in. After he had been with us for a month, on his own, not together with the others, an extra really, his father came to pick him up. He arrived in a car the like of which none of us had ever seen before, so classy. The young man wept and said that he wanted to stay a while longer with us: it was so beautiful here, he was so happy here. So our father said he would take it upon himself to sort something out. The two got on well together, our father and the young man. My father was only slightly older than him, I suspect that when he looked at him, he must have thought to himself, that could have been me, and it almost did happen to me, I was also left lying in the dirt, but I didn't have an army vehicle run over my leg, my leg just got frozen off, I got lucky. The professor and his wife now came to visit more often. Always in their smart car, up the steep hillside.

We children used to help wash the car, I have a vague memory of that. That I dabbed around with my hands on the warm metal. I don't remember the man himself. Or whether he looked like a spirit. Once they stayed almost a whole month. That had also not been planned and was actually not permitted, my father took responsibility for that too. He was the head of the Convalescent Home for War-wounded, he ran the place as it suited him and as he thought fit. He introduced the young man to the other guests as his assistant.

The house was either completely full or empty. Full in summer, June, July, August, and in spring at Easter – from Holy Week up until the Sunday after Easter. At other times, the Home was empty. For two-thirds of the year we were the only ones living there: Father, Mother, Gretel, Richard and I. And the cook. And Lotte, the kitchen help. And the cook's husband moved in at some point, our father had no objection, he took responsibility for that too. The husband was a big help to him, he could turn his hand to almost anything, repairing windows, painting, laying pipes. I was wary of him, he always looked stern. And then our Aunt Irma moved in as well, our mother's younger sister. She had nothing else. Everything she possessed fitted into one suitcase and that couldn't have been very heavy since she had carried it up the mountain to us without any assistance. From then on, Aunt Irma was the chambermaid and our father somehow arranged things so that she received a small wage. He had, said my stepmother, managed to 'wangle it somehow'.

The Home was owned by an association in Stuttgart, Germany. Its members were people of means, exactly what kind of people they were I don't know. Philanthropists, they said. The professor from Tübingen, the humanities academic or 'scientist of the spirit', was a member of this association. Our father had applied for the post of manager or head or caretaker or host – different people called it different things. The distant association placed their trust in him, for he himself was disabled, and his calm manner had, I suspect, made an impression at the interview. A manner that implied everything will be fine. Nothing was more urgently needed than this sort of attitude. Those disabled in the war, who were seeking some fresh summer air or an Easter break, only had to deal with a little bit of bureaucracy, declaring the nature of their disability – you could see it at first glance anyway – before coming up to be well fed and looked after, with evenings of entertainment offered to them and the freshest air imaginable and not a word about the war. Everyone was happy.

On the last day of every session, before the bus came to pick up the guests, a photograph was taken. Erwin Thurnher, the photographer, was not content with taking mere snaps, he was an artist; that's what he wanted to be, an artist, a director.

The young man from Tübingen who was missing one whole arm and half a leg and three-quarters of his mind – I'll call him Ferdinand, I don't know his real name but he should not remain nameless – he was not on any formal paperwork. His father had requested this and he'd requested that he should be especially well treated, like a friend, a good friend. I can remember Ferdinand but not clearly, it's like an out-of-focus photograph, Gretel can remember more about him.

'He was always at Vati's side,' she said. 'They both hobbled along. I can see them in front of me, I just have to close my eyes, they both hobble past the birches, both wearing suits, I imagine them both wearing their Sunday suits …'

'Did he laugh?' I ask.

'What do you mean?'

'Did they laugh together?'

'Why would they have laughed?'

'I just had a vision of them too. Going over the meadow, past the birches, around the house. Both hobbling. And then they realise that they are both hobbling in step and that makes them laugh.'

'That's quite possible,' says Gretel.

We sit there for a while with eyes closed, my sister and I.

Ferdinand's left sleeve is tucked into his jacket pocket, stitched in place, Aunt Irma had taken care of that. He had wavy hair, like Beethoven. Gretel remembers the two of them, he and my father, lying side by side on the terrace in late summer after the last guests had gone, each on one of the red-and-white-striped deckchairs. Both had unfastened their prostheses, which lay beside them within arm's reach, the leather gleaming in the sun, polished by their stumps. Ferdinand coughed because he kept choking on his own spittle and our father was reading aloud to his friend, his good friend. It did not matter what he read, as long as it told of another world. At that time there were still not many books in the Home. The odd book had possibly been left behind by a guest, most of them belonged to us, well-thumbed volumes with damaged spines. *The Adventures of Tom Sawyer* and *The Adventures of Huckleberry Finn*. Or *The Leatherstocking Tales* by James Fenimore Cooper. And of course, *Ivanhoe* by Walter Scott, the book that our father had brought with him from his childhood into the new era. The *Scoundrel Stories* of Ludwig Thoma. *Plish and Plum* by Wilhelm Busch, he particularly liked that one, he knew long passages of it off by heart:

Newly pitched up in this land
His telescope grasped in his hand
Blessed with wealth beyond belief
Came a man, whose name was Pief.
Said he: 'Why should I not, while walking,
Keep into the distance gawking.

It's lovely elsewhere too they say
And I am here now anyway.'

I remember this verse, also that I thought 'telescope' was a kind of small animal that could fit into your hand. Gretel recalls that our mother would often join us and listen while our father read aloud or recited. The others, the cook and her husband and Lotte, sometimes came too, Aunt Irma always.

Those were the reading hours. Aunt Irma would later call them: 'The famous reading hours'. And she would go on to say she was convinced there had never been anything nicer in the whole world, and there never would be anything nicer, and that, all things considered, such a wonderful feeling was worth far more than happiness in love. The truth was, she said, she could not think of heaven being any other way, no priest could persuade her that heaven was better. Either it was exactly like this, or it did not exist: we sit on a terrace looking at the mountain scenery, everything we need and want is there beside us, we only need to stretch out a hand, and we listen to your father, reading aloud from his books. Our father, she said, had a voice that could have earned him a fortune, if he could only have been persuaded. Why had he never thought, for example, of becoming a radio presenter, she could not understand it! In this wonderful air, on this wonderful terrace, with this wonderful stillness, they had sat in these wonderful deckchairs side by side, had drunk hot chocolate with a blob of whipped cream on top, and with it, something that really didn't go with it but was the best thing ever, a piece of bread and ham, and our father had read aloud until it got dark and too chilly to sit outside. 'You were still in the bassinet. I used to jiggle you,' said Aunt Irma to me in dialect. 'Jiggling' meant rocking the cradle till the baby fell asleep. Back inside the dining hall the young man from Tübingen would push and pull a bit on the accordion, she added, and who knows, perhaps he remembered that before the war he used to play the violin; at any rate no one said it sounded terrible or nothing like music. I think, by the way, that Aunt Irma is a little confused here: I was too big for the bassinet by then. She is probably thinking of our brother, Richard. I can remember the reading hours, not clearly, but if I'd had the words, I too would have said: this is happiness. This word, it seems to me, comes into its own only once its opposite has made an appearance. Then one remembers what things were like before. And another thing: I ask myself how Ferdinand is supposed to have played the accordion when he was missing an arm. Aunt Irma was imagining a bit too much happiness.

Everyone knew that the reading hours were meant for Ferdinand. Everyone knew that this was how our father kept the promise he had given to the professor from Tübingen to treat his son like a good friend and not just like any other guest.

Ferdinand was with us for a year, then his father took him back home. His wife had died and he could not bear being alone, he wanted something to occupy him. Not long after, Ferdinand died too. He was not yet thirty years old. Up until his death he spoke again and again of the reading hours on the Tschengla and how he wished he could be part of that once more.

And now pay attention! – Before the professor himself died a short time later, he bequeathed parts of his library to the Convalescent Home for War-wounded. Expressly. That's what it said in the will. Each book title was listed separately. That must have taken him a lot of time and energy. So he had given a lot of thought to it. And considering the titles and the authors, it's fair to conclude that he did not intend the books to be solely and exclusively for the entertainment and recreation of the war victims, for in that case there would be no Kant among them, no Fichte nor Darwin nor the endless rows of classics, Plato's *Republic* and the essays of Montaigne and Francis Bacon. Quite the opposite: no light reading was included. No Karl May, no Hedwig Courths-Mahler. I have the impression he selected books that his son, had there been no war, should have read. Those he would have given his son to read. That he had bequeathed the books to the Home was thanks to my father. Who else could take the credit? He was the one who had performed the readings. He had read aloud to Ferdinand and given him some memorable times after the war took everything from him, one arm right up to his armpit, half his left leg and three-quarters of his mind – such a fine mind it had been. For this the professor wanted to show his gratitude. To our father. Who could possibly think otherwise?

'How do you know all that?' asked my stepmother. 'Were you there? Did you see the professor's will?'

'Vati told me,' I said, and although I tried to hide it, my voice sounded petulant. As if I were lying.

'Your father,' she said, 'told me as well. Exactly like that. The same story.'

'Well then,' I said.

'But neither of us knows if it's true.'

The Home was built of wood and looked imposing, it had nothing of the alpine hut about it; it looked like an English country house. It lay in a dip, was extensive and had an upper floor. I have a feeling I saw a similar one in an Agatha Christie film. At the entrance was a porch, as I mentioned before, supported by two wooden pillars carved in a spiral design. There were two front doors, the inner had little honeycomb stained-glass windows, the panes set in delicate wooden frames, a golden light streamed through them. The outside door was removed from its hinges during the warmer months, a heavy oak door that was supposed to withstand the winter storms that often hurled more than a metre of snow against the house. The back of the house faced south, that's where the terrace was, I would guess it was twelve metres long and five metres wide. Wood decking made of larch, silvered by the weather. There was room for up to thirty deckchairs. Beside each one a little table for drinks, books or a newspaper. The sort of tables that have a base made of bamboo. Among them, parasols advertising Almdudler soft drinks. From here you could see far down into the valley and over to the mountains on the other side, where the snowfields glittered all year round. The veranda continued on round the narrow sides of the house, so we had sun all day. The window frames were clean and white, the wood on the facades weathered to shades of brown and black by the sun.

There were actually only two rooms assigned to the manager and his family: a bedroom and a living room-cum-kitchen. My father requisitioned two more rooms from the ones that faced north, the less desirable ones, so that we now had our own separate living room and a bedroom for my sister and me. Baby Richard slept with his parents. Downstairs leading through to the terrace was a large dining hall, the walls panelled with wood, not in rustic fashion but highly polished like on a luxurious sailing boat, as were the two round wooden pillars in the middle.

On one wall in the dining hall hung a huge oil painting. It portrayed the fairy tale 'The Seven

Swabians'. They are messing about with a spear, making the most idiotic faces. They stand in a line, hiding one behind the other. I do a search on Google for 'Seven Swabians', click on 'images', and with a tap on the appropriate key, the picture materialises. My heart skips a beat! I recognise every detail. I read that the picture is from a postcard series by the painter Georg Mühlberg. An artist must therefore have copied it from this small format onto a canvas two metres by one metre; the painting must have been a gift to the Convalescent Home for War-wounded when it was founded, from a grateful donor – just like the donor of our library. I know the story of the stupid Swabians very well, it comes from the Brothers Grimm, and our father read it aloud to us often enough. Each time we all laughed a lot. It made us laugh even harder that he did not laugh. When one of us burst into fits, he stopped reading and looked at the offender so seriously, the rest of us lost control. 'Well begun is half done!' In the end, he couldn't open his mouth to finish the story without us laughing. The stupid Swabians, Master Schulz, Jackli, Marli, Jergli, Michal, Hans and Veitli got hold of a spear so they could fight a monster, which turned out to be a terrified hare.

The kitchen with its modern fittings was next to the dining hall, divided from it by a frosted-glass sliding door. Later, shortly before we moved away, we even got a fridge, which was so tall that my sister and

I could only reach the top two compartments if we stood on a stool. In the top compartment were the glass jars of luscious fruit conserves, cherries, pears – each one with a stick of cinnamon – and apple purée.

The library was at the very back of the house, facing north-east. A mighty fir tree grew in front of it. When my father opened the window, the smell of resin drifted in and mingled with the musty smell of the books – for me today still a scent from paradise.

To the north were the mountains and the forest. Dark fir-tree forest. I didn't like it. For me it was the enemy at the gate. I liked the smell of the forest but only at its edge. And we were happy playing at the edge. In summer you could feel that certain warmth that can only be felt at the edge of a forest, as if something was about to burst into flame. I loved that and still love it today. Our father often went hiking through the forest, always on his own, sometimes he set off straight after breakfast and did not return until the evening. Then he collapsed into the leather armchair beside the hearth in the dining hall, flipped the cap off a bottle of beer with his thumb, unfastened his prosthesis, often it would be bloody, and our mother would rub ointment over his stump. He'd come back from the forest with a sack over his shoulder, bits of twig in his hair, his rucksack full of beetles and plants. The beetles he put into jam jars and tied a scrap of fabric over the top with string – he had cut the rounds of fabric from dish towels the day before. In the evening, with the lamp pulled down low, he pinned the beetles onto a wooden board covered with black velvet, cut strips of white card with the scissors, wrote on them with India ink and stuck the labels under the respective samples. Sometimes he asked if we children wanted to come with him into the forest. We didn't. Our mother didn't want to either. Even though she would have been well equipped for a hike – walking boots, ski pants with a band of elastic under the foot to keep the legs from riding up out of her boots. She also had a thick, red-and-black-checked flannel shirt. And a walking stick. Lotte would have loved to accompany him, but she was never asked. My father was quite happy to be alone for a whole day in the forest.

June, July, August, that is when the guests came. And in Holy Week and up until the Sunday after Easter. That made a pleasant change. One-legged, one-armed men, men with coughs, men in wheel-chairs, some one-eyed with pirate eyepatches, blind men with white sticks, some mentally impaired, the lost, abandoned, forgotten. Those whom people would rather not see. Because they were a reminder of the war. They stood in the way. With us they could enjoy themselves. With us there was always something going on, and we children allowed them to poke fun at us. No evening without a sing-song. And we were allowed to stay up late. Even when we had to go to school the next day, half an hour down the mountain and one and a half hours back up again.

Gretel and I still laugh when we remember what a bad cook our mother was. She was no good at it; really, she had no need to be good at it. We had a cook. Our mother did not take care of the household. Not the essential things anyway. 'Essential' was what Aunt Irma deemed essential. And she was always right. The shopping list was essential, it was for the cook's husband, who was responsible for the purchasing, once a week he borrowed a van and brought up the things Aunt Irma had requested. Organising the washing days was essential. Sorting out a supply of firewood in good time was essential. And who supervised Gretel's and my homework? Aunt Irma.

Our mother looked after the non-essential. The deer for example. So that when it was cold and snowing they were given their heads of cabbage. It seemed like the cabbage was meant only for the deer. None of us liked cabbage, not even Aunt Irma, but as a hangover from the war days she felt one must always have cabbage to hand, so she would write down cabbage on the shopping list. Flour and cabbage. Just the smell of it made me feel ill. It still has that effect on me today. In the early days, whenever my husband used to cook *Fleckerl* pasta squares with cabbage in the pan, I would say, just a small portion for me, please. Now he knows. The deer loved cabbage. Our mother knew that. She used to speak to the deer;

from a distance I saw how the animals stood at the edge of the forest in the deep snow and waited for her, so trusting that they ate out of her hand. No one believes me but I saw it with my own eyes. I saw our mother's lips moving, speaking to the deer. When people speak to animals, they usually use baby talk. Our mother didn't speak to the deer that way. You could see that even from far off. The deer looked at her attentively.

I asked her: 'What did you say to them today?'

Her gaze brushed over me. 'Oh, leave off,' was all she said.

'No,' I said. 'I really want to know.'

'Goodness me! The normal sort of stuff people chat about.'

Our mother seldom chatted with people. She used to sit on one side, listen or pretend to be listening, or else she had developed a listening face over the course of her life so that she didn't have to make an effort any more. Sometimes in the night I would hear my parents having a conversation. Then both of them would be talking and they talked a lot.

I'd wake Gretel and say: 'They're talking again.'

And we strained our ears to hear.

Our mother also cared for all the birds, gave them a piece of butter and the best grains, kneaded the grains into the butter. She would never have given the birds margarine. Our father hated margarine too, margarine and malt coffee; he wanted strong, black, freshly ground coffee. He had his own cup. A small coffee house cup. Maybe he had pocketed it some place or other. Quite a few of our guests preferred margarine to butter. The margarine came from the shop and was in a packet, the butter we bought direct from the farmer, you could see fingerprints on it, some found that disgusting.

I think Aunt Irma put the fear of God into our mother. Sometimes Aunt Irma would run her finger over a surface, look at her finger and say: 'This needs another going over.'

When the guests had left, we had the huge house to ourselves again.

A rowan tree with red berries grew in front of our kitchen window, a mountain ash some people call it. The berries were poisonous, they were used for making schnapps. Aunt Irma used to make a compote out of them and bottle it. As medicine. For a sore throat or a pain in the stomach. Our father said this was nonsense and dangerous. For a sore throat the best thing was aspirin and for a stomach ache a laxative. How the two of them used to fight about that. Why do I mention the rowan tree? Let me put it like this: it makes me feel emotional. On my daily stroll across the Schlossberg I walk past one. When it is loaded with berries, its branches bow down across the path. It always makes me think of our mother. And I get these childish notions, for someone of my age childish notions: that she has turned into the tree in front of our kitchen window on the Tschengla. That the tree has absorbed her into itself.

One day our father came up from the valley with a film projector. He had borrowed it from the union for the season when we had guests. In the evening a linen sheet was draped over the painting of the Seven Swabians in the dining hall, the tables were pushed to one side, the chairs arranged in rows. And then we played at going to the cinema. I remember only one film clearly: *Vulture Wally*. I remember another film but only the first sentence, spoken by a male voice: 'A ship arrived in the port of Kavala with thousands of mules on board …' There came a point where everyone had seen every film or even seen them twice, and soon only Gretel and I were the only ones left in the dining hall, the disabled guests sat on the terrace and played cards, it was, after all, summer and still light and warm at ten o'clock. I only wanted to watch *Vulture Wally*, the other films were of no interest to me. Soon Gretel too had had enough. Towards the end of the season my father was setting up the cinema just for me. Yes, just for me he arranged thirty seats, all lined up in rows, to make me feel as if I were sitting in a cinema. And it always gave me a thrill. I could not get enough of Wally and Bear-Josef, I liked Afra too, although night after night I felt the same anger towards her, even though I knew she was not Josef's new lover but his niece. I could sit down in front of the screen as if I'd never seen the film before, though I had seen it ten times. My father came up behind me and stroked the hair off my forehead. He had a few tender gestures in reserve, tender words none, at any rate not for his children. Then he went to join the others on the terrace and left me alone with the men and women on the screen, who did the same things and said the same things every evening but each time as if it were new. I raged like Wally, wished death on Josef, I loved the vulture that Wally reared, even though he had wings like the wings of the eagle that I feared so much …

I fall into daydreaming again and see the colours of the Tschengla: lily white, gentian blue, strawberry red. Every day I walk across the mountain known as the Schlossberg, where my daughter had her fall, she was twenty-one, just newly twenty-one. I told her stories about the Tschengla so often. 'Mama, tell me about when you were little!' And always I see the two police officers in front of me, a woman and a man, who had come through the garden gate; they had seen me out in the garden from the street, cutting roses. I sink to my knees in the grass and see the accident, even before they say the word.

'Is she dead?' I stammer. The policeman puts a hand to his face, the policewoman says: 'She's been taken to hospital by helicopter, she's undergoing an emergency operation.' They've still not said her name.

Paula was going hiking on the mountain that morning with a girlfriend. Climbing, said her friend, adding, I know the area really well, there's a fantastic steep track up, we'll go that way.

'You're not going to go in those shoes!' I say.

Paula gives me a look: 'Mama, we're going walking, nothing serious.'

Her trainers were yellow. My husband and I buried them under an apple tree on the Schlossberg. Because you have to do something, the days are so awful, so awfully long, when someone is missing. One has to do something, something that feels symbolic, or like a ritual, otherwise one doesn't know how one can bear it.

I can't bear to look at idyllic things. I can't even think about them. I don't want to. They always seem to shatter instantly. I have a sense of relief when I come across something unexpectedly ugly, crouching in a corner, grinning and taunting: you see, there is no such thing as absolute beauty. I know of few things more beautiful than the rowan tree. A magnificent one grows on the Schlossberg over the path. I quicken my pace there.

Not only did the cook's husband have a driving licence, he could do repairs too. For example, he repaired the little cargo cable car that had been built before the war. Probably for the loggers. The Home did not even exist at that time. Apparently the man operating it died, and after the war, no one was responsible for anything anyway, no one looked after the cable car and it fell into disrepair. As time went on, it would surely turn to rust and crumble into the earth, the cables would break and cause damage. So my father and the cook's husband took it over, treated the lift as if it belonged to the Convalescent Home for War-wounded. For the Home the renovation was a big improvement. It made good sense. No one could dispute that. From now on, no one would have to cart heavy things up the valley on their back. Technology would take over. To transport passengers in the cable car was strictly forbidden. But sometimes my sister and I were allowed to travel on it. Gretel was scared, I wasn't.

Even today Gretel says: 'Can you imagine what might have happened! That was irresponsible of Vati! I am convinced Mutti didn't know about it. What on earth was he thinking! As I remember, we didn't even want to. I didn't anyway. Honestly, that's right, he persuaded us. It's unbelievable! The cable cars weren't really cars, they had no bars, there were just a few boards nailed together, hanging from four chains – rusty ones! And in one place, the cable ran over a gorge. We would have been dead! I could still get worked up about it even today!'

I say: 'You already are.'

'We could have been dead, for God's sake!'

'I loved doing it! I could have done it again and again!'

'Yeah, sure!'

'Do you regret doing it?'

Gretel ponders a moment and her mouth twists into a grin: 'No, I'd do it again too. But only if you came with me.'

'I would!'

Eventually it was made into a proper cable car. With two gondolas each carrying five people, proper gondolas that complied with safety rules. The mayor of the district to which the Tschengla belonged had taken the project in hand. Under construction for a good six months. Times were better and were supposed to get better still. And they turned out even better than people had hoped. We acquired a telephone. No one had expected that. The line was laid all the way up to us, it was done at the same time as the construction of the new cable car. The telephone hung on the wall in the dining hall. We had a telephone and didn't know anyone to call. Nor did we receive any calls. For a long time. One day I was skipping through the dining hall when it rang. We had already practised just for fun. I picked up the receiver and said: 'Hello? This is the Convalescent Home for War-wounded speaking.' It was my Uncle Lorenz whom at that time I had not yet met in person. He asked who I was. I said: 'It's Monika.' – 'Aha,' he said. Was Papa nearby? I put the telephone back on its cradle, because I thought that was the correct thing to do, and ran outside and called my father. The telephone rang again a few minutes later.

In addition to our clients, summer holidaymakers now came to the mountain, non-disabled, normal tourists, mainly from Germany but also from Vienna. They rented rooms in one of the farmhouses in the area for one or two weeks, went hiking, praised the hospitality, returned home and recommended the area to others. The new cable car was intended for these people. The idea was that they could ride down to the valley now and again for some shopping. Among these summer visitors, we heard, were distinguished, wealthy people, doctors, lawyers, men in important positions accompanied by their wives, men who were contacted for advice even when on holiday. Often, calls came in, could we pass on a message to this person or that person who was holidaying in this or that house. Many of these people owned their own holiday home, a new build or a refurbished old house. Gretel and I would deliver the messages. We liked doing that, there was a tip, fifty groschen and hopefully some nut cake. We used to knock on the front door and call out: 'Telephone message!' The husband or the wife would appear, and we would hand over the slip with the name of the person who had called written on it. Aunt Irma had written the note – the name of the caller, plus a few key words explaining what the call was about. She had the most beautiful handwriting and she wrote without any errors. She was quite conceited about this. Aunt Irma was in charge of 'overall management of operations', she was our father's 'right hand', a sort of secretary and staff supervisor on top of her duties as chambermaid, and therefore senior even to the cook and her husband, and to Lotte. 'Chambermaid' was just the job title on her wage slip.

The gondolas on the new cable car were made of aluminium and flashed when the sun fell on them, brand spanking new they were, a symbol for a brand spanking new age. You could see even from a distance − look, that's something new! As soon as the season was over, the lift stopped operating. Our father however was given a key. It was conceded that the Home needed a lot of supplies and that one should be supportive of the war-wounded and not be penny-pinching, even though the Convalescent Home for War-wounded was not an Austrian organisation but a German one, and more to the point a Swabian one. So in emergencies our father was allowed to use the cable car. Such an emergency was very rare. Once when a woman from the neighbourhood went into labour early. Another time when a logger injured himself badly. But also when Gretel and I made incessant appeals and gazed at him with pleading eyes. We would get into one of the gondolas, ride down and back up again. If we saw anyone, we had to tuck ourselves out of sight. And if anyone ever raised the subject, we were supposed to deny everything.

'It was only once,' said Gretel.

'No,' I say, 'at least three times.'

'Once,' she says.

'Three times,' I say.

Together we look at one of the old photographs. Gretel is sitting on a toboggan, I am standing beside her. I am pouting, I wanted the photo to make me look like one of the sophisticated women in the illustrated magazines that lay around in the dining hall for the guests.

And then, on the day the photographer set up his camera on a tripod to take pictures of us and the disabled guests, the two men arrived. Who had never been here before. They had driven up in an Opel Rekord, a light grey one with a soft top. With German number plates. While we were lining up for the photographer, they were inspecting the house …

The sad story that now follows has a backstory, which shows how a senseless thing can be set in motion. And this is the backstory:

It happened in winter. The telephone rang, again I picked up, a man was on the line, could he speak to the manager. This time I didn't hang up. The man was calling from Stuttgart, he was someone from the association to which our Home belonged, maybe even its president. He was letting us know that he was about to pay a visit. And visit he did, a few days later. A small man with no visible neck, very short arms, very short legs. He had brought something with him for everyone, *Lebkuchen* biscuits decorated with brightly coloured icing. He said that good times were on the way for us, different times, better times to be exact. That looking to the future an establishment like this could not continue operating for only three or four months in the year and staying empty the rest of the time, that was simply not viable any longer. First of all, it would be a shame, and secondly, it would be a waste. The convalescence sessions for war-wounded men would of course continue to be provided as before, more effectively and with better equipment, though obviously not in the best summer months, but in the in-between seasons, that is autumn and winter. The disabled were less reliant on the weather. In the remaining months however, the house would not be left standing empty but would be run as a hotel or bed-and-breakfast business, for a profit; people were happy to pay good money for these surroundings and this air. My father would of course continue to be the manager, and now the hotel manager, and he could naturally expect a hefty increase in salary. To a great extent things would remain much as they were, everything else however would change.

Firstly, he said, the house had to be adapted, that is, reconstructed. More rooms. Might even be necessary to add an extension. The man asked for a tour of the house and made various comments.

'What's in this room?'

'The library,' said my father.

'A library?'

'Yes.'

'Really, you have a library up here?'

'Yes,' said my father proudly. 'Would you like to see it?'

The man did not want to. He just cast a glance inside. The light was not even switched on. You could make two cosy little bedrooms out of that, he said. Research had shown that people from the city who travel to the mountains for a holiday prefer small, cramped, cosy rooms, somewhere rustic, a sort of nest if you like.

And what would happen to the books then? asked my father.

'To the books?' said the man. People did not come up here to spend time reading. Otherwise they might just as well stay down below. Reading meant staring at a book, up here anyone with any sense wanted to look at the mountains. 'Up here people want to sunbathe and go for walks. To enjoy nature, not huddle indoors.' Was the so-called library used very frequently?

My father had to admit that it was not.

'Well then,' said the man. 'What's to be done?' It was as if he expected our father to give the same answer that he himself would have given if asked.

It was from that moment that my father began to break up the library. My stepmother called it 'stashing away'. I say: he was saving the books.

I mentioned already that during this time he was attending night school to study for the Matura exam. That he was down in the town in the valley once a week, where he had rented a small room; the money came this time not from the church but from the trade union, a stipend. The courses were scheduled intensively over two days. Friday evening the first lecture, on Saturday from morning to evening one class after another, and then on Sunday morning as well. From now on, our father left the Home at midday on Friday with two full suitcases and returned on Sunday afternoon with two empty ones. He piled up the books in his little room. He had no idea how this was going to pan out. His plan after the Matura exam was to continue studying, preferably chemistry, then to move into the town with his family, find a good job, rent an apartment large enough to have one room as a library, following the example of the master builder from Mariapfarr in Lungau. He believed that no one knew precisely how many books there were in the Convalescent Home for War-wounded. He believed that no one would ever find him out. No, really, he was even doing the association a favour, the future did not belong to those who just sit on their hands. He did not yet know that the professor from Tübingen had itemised every book he wanted to donate to the Home in his will. And so he felt confident in his belief that he was the only person who had a detailed knowledge of the books. He did not want to stash away every single book. That would have been too obvious. But he wanted to save about five to six hundred of the most beautiful, most interesting and most valuable books. The others would unfortunately just have to be sacrificed. Either carted off to an antiquarian dealer at a price per kilo or to a flea market or sent for pulping.

And then, after Easter, once again a surprise call from Stuttgart: the following day two men would be coming, an architect and the association's auditor. The house was to be surveyed for the reconstruction and possible extension. In addition, an assessment of the assets would be made, an inventory in other words. And now that the guests would soon be gone, a start could be made on the clearing out. Time is money, and money is progress, and progress is clearly good. The guest house or hotel business was to start this coming summer. Bookings were already being taken for the disabled sessions in autumn and winter.

There were however around two hundred books that still needed to be saved, the beautiful Kant volumes for example. Take them to the flea market? Or the three-volume, richly illustrated edition by Achim von Arnim and Clemens Brentano of *Des Knaben Wunderhorn* (*The Boy's Magic Horn*) – to the recycling? Or the magnificent edition of *Don*

Quixote, illustrated by Gustave Doré – down into a deep cellar to be eaten by mould? But there was no time to pack the cases and go down to the town and store the books out of harm's way in his little room.

I admit it, these are my own conjectures, mine alone. How could I have any idea what our father was thinking? Whichever angle I look at it from, it always adds up to the same senseless outcome.

What did he actually do? He wrapped in waxed cloth the remaining books that he wanted to save; six large packets, in waxed tablecloths from the kitchen that were spread over the dining tables during the session – there were some disabled guests who shook uncontrollably and it would have been too much work to wash the tablecloths after every single meal, breakfast, lunch and dinner. He tied the parcels up in watertight bundles and then he called for me. I was to give him a hand …

All of this is a puzzle to me! Why me? I have never discussed this with Gretel and definitely not with our stepmother. Not with anyone. Only with my husband. What did my father want from me? He did not really need me, he could have managed on his own. There were six packages, each one far too heavy for me to lift or carry. He got the wheelbarrow out of the shed, loaded two packages into it and pushed the lot up to the edge of the forest.

I walked along beside him. 'What are you doing?' I asked him.

Then the next trip, another two packages. And then the last two. He set them down one after the other at the edge of the forest, behind the bushes, so they couldn't be seen from the house. There was no one there anyway.

I carried on walking beside him, kept asking him: 'What's going on? Why are you doing this? Why are we doing this?'

His answer: 'You'll see soon enough. Don't ask me again!'

He had fixed it so no one was in the Home that day. Just him and me. The others had taken Richard for a walk in the pram. Or had gone to visit someone. I don't know, they weren't there. Finally, he fetched a pick and shovel out of the shed, pressed the shovel into my hand and from the edge of the woods dragged one pack of books after the other further into the forest, to a spot where a fallen tree lay, whose roots had been torn out of the earth. Under the root ball was a hollow so big I could have hidden inside it. There he stacked the packages of books, and then used the pick to loosen the earth, and with the shovel, piled soil over the packages.

I helped him with my bare hands. And I asked again: 'Why are we doing this?'

'This is our treasure,' he said. 'Treasure gets buried. That's the best thing for treasure. Don't forget this spot! Take careful note of where our treasure lies!'

'And who am I allowed to tell?'

'No one.'

'Not even Gretel?'

'No.'

'Not even Mutti?'

'No one means no one. Repeat after me!'

'No one means no one. And when will we dig the treasure up again?'

'One day.'

'Soon?'

'Yes, soon.'

We piled dead leaves and small twigs over the fresh earth, it looked as if it had always been like that. No treasure to be seen anywhere. Suddenly he raised his head, looked up at the treetops and ran off. Leaving me standing. In the middle of the forest. I saw him running. Hopping, to be more precise. He dragged the leg with the prosthesis behind him. I saw him running with arms bent and could hear him panting through the forest. In the same rhythm as the movement of his arms. Like children do when someone calls them and they know they're going to be in for it. And I was the cool-headed one. I knew what needed to be done, hid the wheelbarrow and the tools in the shed. While my father lay down on the sofa in the sitting room with his clothes and shoes still on and fell asleep on the spot. And could not be woken. Slept until the others came back from their walk or wherever it was they had been.

Is that not strange? All of that? It's difficult to get one's head around!

This story comes back to me time and time again. And it is actually just the backstory. My father buried the books and he could have managed it all on his own, but he wanted me to be there. Why and why me? That's the strangest part. Richard was a baby, still in his cradle. Probably my father would have preferred to bury the treasure with a son as witness rather than a daughter. Gretel was the oldest. Why not her? He wanted me with him. Me, my father's buddy. There was a time when I found this thought nauseating. And there was a time when I felt proud when I thought of it. It must be, I mused, because he considered me to be the only one of his children that he felt he could trust to look after the treasure. It was like a minor subplot from the legends of King Arthur or some such tale – 'The Guardian of the Treasure'. Afterwards my father and I never talked about it again. Sometime later, when the world, and indeed our lives too, had completely changed, he asked me – I was eighteen or younger – what I hoped for in life. I answered, and this was not just to make him happy, it was the truth: 'I hope that one day my name will appear on the spine of a book.'

Why had he involved me in this? Did he want there to be someone who knew where the treasure was buried – once he was gone? Was the thought of wanting to 'do away with himself' already there in his head – should he be found out? This makes me think of our brother, Richard. He lived from day to day. He never worried. He had never had a plan. Day after day. Year after year. Without a purpose. Without a goal. Even at school so many girls were in love with him. And later so many women. And that was because he never made any effort. He never chased after any girl. He didn't put himself out for any of them. He didn't bother about his appearance. And he never gave any thought to what pick-up lines to use. Everything came easy to him, he always took things easy. When he stank like a polecat because he'd been out on the prowl for two days and two nights, smoking marijuana and drinking beer and lounging about in airless rooms, he'd lie down in the bath in hot water, without soap, without shampoo, he simply lay down in the bath and stayed there until the water got cold. Then out, and without drying himself off, pulled his old clothes on again. He used to say: 'If it all goes pear-shaped, there's always the option of suicide.' And in the end, that's what he did. I suspect that my father had exactly the same idea. And that this thought had in fact been with him since childhood: if everything goes pear-shaped, there's always the option of suicide. Or as the legendary wit Nestroy says: 'If I reach the end of my tether, I'll string myself up.'

And then he came to the conclusion that he had now reached the end of his tether. The two men from Stuttgart came as announced, the auditor of the association and the architect. It so happened that at the same time as they were coming up the gravel road to us, the bus that was to pick up our guests was driving up behind them. The session had come to an end. The photographer was already waiting, the disabled men were already waiting. The bus driver was also supposed to be in the picture and was waiting in anticipation. He had never yet been missing from any of the pictures. A section of the bus had to be in there too. The back part with the crooked ladder up to the roof where the suitcases were tied down. The gentlemen from Stuttgart, both in sleeveless pullovers with a diamond pattern, with similar ties, the top button of their shirts undone, both with horn-rimmed glasses. Like twins they looked, and yet, as they told us, they had only met for the first time on the journey over here; they were very friendly, greeted everyone with a handshake, said, please don't go to any trouble, a glass of water and a coffee would be fine. Down in the valley they had settled themselves into a guest house, they would be staying for at most one or two, or at the outside three hours.

Our father joined them on the veranda.

One of them, the auditor, opened his briefcase and said: 'I have here a list of all the things, ah, yes, all the bits and pieces that, you know, the association has supplied during the years, just for form's sake, so that we have an overview. A sort of inventory. I imagine half the things are no longer of any use, we'll have to get some new ones. If you could say what belongs to you and your family. If it's not inconvenient, then I could just have a quick look around and get an overview of things.'

He put down his documents in front of our father, if the skimpy papers could even be called documents. 'It's all just a formality.' To comply with the statutes of the association. Would my father care to look through them, please, that would make his task easier, said the gentleman. And then my father spotted the list of books that the professor from Tübingen had donated to the Convalescent Home for War-wounded. An impressive list, meticulously organised by subject matter – philosophy, history, literature, science – in alphabetical order by author. Attached to the list was the relevant paragraph from the will, certified with a notary's signature and stamp. All the other documents consisted of various notes, most of them handwritten – a hasty inventory of kitchen equipment, a stock count of bedlinen and curtains, tools and so on. Only the list of books had an official air about it. And for that reason seemed of more importance than everything else. My father knew – or thought he knew – that the auditor would be focusing his attention mainly on this list. To make the journey all the way from Stuttgart, Germany, to the Austrian mountains just because of those few other files would have been sheer stupidity and not worth the cost of the fuel.

He would have to present something to the association, some kind of assessment, regardless of what
value he, the auditor, ascribed to the library; for the
only document in his briefcase worthy of the name
was the list of books the professor from Tübingen
had handed over to the notary before his death, and
that was that. So our father knew – or thought he
knew – that they would find him out. That he would
be called a thief. A swindler. That they would throw
him out. Dismissed. Without notice. No more talk
of hotel manager. That he would be charged. As my
stepmother said: the Germans don't mess around.
That we would have to move out. Theft. As our
stepmother said: even worse, the theft of something
intended for the poorest of the poor, regardless of
whether these poorest of the poor had any interest
in it or not. He would have been ruined. *We* would
have been ruined. Finished. A destroyed family.

He heard someone calling him. The war-wounded
were waiting, the photographer was waiting. The
bus driver was waiting. They wanted to finish taking
the picture. The two gentlemen from Stuttgart said
he should feel free to go ahead, they would find
everything they needed on their own. There was no
subtext to this, no lack of trust. What likelihood was
there of any impropriety up here?

'You go ahead, we'll manage!'

And now everything is frozen in one image. The
photographer arranges the disabled men in front of

the Convalescent Home for War-wounded. In the background, the birches and the spiral pillars at the front door. The war veterans quickly run their fingers through their hair, one doesn't want to let the side down. One spits on his comb, another just needs a minute to put on a clean shirt.

'Who's going to be able to see that you stink! You can stink without a qualm on a photo.'

All the others: 'Ha, ha, ha, ha!'

Him: 'Well, I still stink, but at least the shirt doesn't.'

All the others: 'Ha, ha, ha, ha!'

A third secretly takes off his braces and tucks them into his trouser pocket, he wants to wear only a belt and not belt and braces, or one day someone will look at the photo and laugh at him: 'That one there must have been a real wimp, that's why he got shot and wounded in the war rather than shot dead!' – that's not what he wants.

The women put on white aprons and tie them around their waists. Lotte has a bowl and a whisk on her knees and pretends to be stirring something.

'Are we going to have a farewell pudding?'

Lotte: 'No, just so no one can say we're slacking off.'

'Not slacking off nearly enough!' shouts someone outside the picture.

Lotte: 'What's that supposed to mean?'

'Do I have to spell it out?'

'Ha, ha, ha, ha!'

Some men sit in the front row on chairs, that is part of the set-up, that's what the photographer wants.

They are to sit so that the person in front provides cover to the person behind. So that the prostheses are not visible and one can't see that here an arm is missing, there a leg. The one with the pirate eyepatch though wants it to be clearly visible.

'Fine, whatever you say, then stand up! Turn towards the right! Or no, better towards the left.'

My mother stands next to our frail-looking father, who looks quite different from everyone else: his face pale, his hair combed back from his high forehead, his eyes half closed. The jacket is two sizes too small, only the top button done up, like Charlie Chaplin, his sleeves too short, you can see his white hands with his piano fingers, as my mother called them, although my father never had anything to do with pianos. His trousers on the other hand are too baggy, also just like Charlie Chaplin, one size too big. The waistband is far too high up. Folded over twice. He is a small man.

'All men were small in those days,' says my husband. He says: 'Your father looks like the young Mao Zedong.'

'You're not the only one to say that,' I say.

'Inner values were highly regarded back then,' says my husband.

I say: 'My father was clearly someone who knew all there was to know about depth. He'd have had trouble fending off even a single punch. Two consecutive punches would have killed him. And yet everyone, whether bulls or bullocks, showed him respect.'

'Ha, depth,' says my husband.

'Because he had depth, yes,' I say.

My husband and my father got on well together. It began when my father first said to him – at that point we were not yet married – that he could go ahead and take one of the books from the shelves, and my husband held it in his hands, the way I had warned him he must do without fail – and please don't do it any other way, treat it carefully, reverently, tenderly as if it were a living thing.

Right at the front stand Gretel and I. And then in front of all of us, in the centre of the picture, the accordion player, he's crouching down on the ground, his right hand on the keys, his left hand on the bass buttons, the bellows opened wide. I know he could not play at all. The photographer had fetched the instrument from the dining hall and pressed it into his chest and arranged his arms and fingers. The man did not even know how to hold the thing.

'Give us a tune!' said the photographer to the man. 'That looks good. You look the part. Now it looks like everyone's having fun.'

'Why me, why does it have to be me?' protested the man with the bad teeth and the traditional jacket, you can see in the photo that he stinks, 'and I don't even have the faintest idea about music, not surprisingly!'

'No one is going to hear you, they'll just see you. No one will know that you can't play.'

The others: 'Ha, ha, ha!'

The man knew they only wanted to have someone to laugh at, not only now but for the next twenty years and even after his death: the one in the front is Gernot, he's the one playing the accordion, though of all of us he was the one with the least idea about music. The photographer pushed and pummelled the man into shape for the picture. Even we children felt sorry for him. He squashed him down, bent his right arm one way, the left another, tilted his neck slightly, mouth open, not so wide or try closed, no, actually better open. He was to make himself small. 'Crouch down!' He was not to hide Gretel and me. 'Down a bit more!' Children are the future after all.

'Hey! Where's Josef?' shouts the photographer.

Our father has disappeared. Where is he? We can't have that! The manager has to be in it. Ah, here he is! He was to go and stand at the side. There was no time to rearrange everything now.

Eventually we were all in place and the photographer clicked the button.

'Well then,' said my stepmother once more. 'What do you think is going through his mind at this point?'

I slide the photograph over to her. As she slides her cigarettes over to me. She knows that I don't smoke any more but would be happy if I made an exception. I would have liked to turn the picture over, I didn't want to look at it any more.

'That same day,' said my stepmother, 'he slipped into the shed, where he always did his experiments, into his laboratory, no one had the slightest idea what he did in there; this time he mixed poison for himself and drank the lot. That's what he told me. His words.'

Lotte was the one who found him. At nine o'clock in the evening.

She wanted to fetch some turpentine for cleaning. That's what she said. That's how she found him. She had noticed that he had not appeared at supper. She knew that he liked going to the shed but not what he did there. Experiments. She wanted to drop in on him, made the pretext she needed turpentine: would he perhaps have some? She had been told that he might have some. What he meant by 'experiments' was of no interest to her. But *he* interested her. His air of absent-mindedness let her imagine all kinds of things about him. Depth in other words. She, with her fawn hair that would not be tamed, kept a watchful eye on our father. All the time. She never dared to say what she was thinking: she wanted him. Three words she could not bring herself to say aloud. Later, songs will be sung with these words as the title. And his wife, who was there and yet not there, who was as distant as if she were a million miles away – did she see anything at all of what was going on around her? Her gaze like his was turned inwards, and when she held baby Richard on her lap and stroked his soft hair, it looked as if she was unaware of what her hands were doing. And what happened when she lay beside her husband at night? Did she know what her hands were doing when they touched him? And what did they say to each other, his face close to hers, her face close to his? And what did he see when he looked into his wife's eyes? More than once, I had noticed how Lotte looked at my mother. No anger, no jealousy, none of those wild flare-ups that went through the head of Vulture Wally that I would have found terrifying, but at the same time exciting. I had seen only two or three films but had already read a pile of books. My mother's eyes follow her husband and she thinks to herself that she knows so little about him. And I know so little about her. In these memories she comes across as such a quiet person; that's not what I want, that's not how she was. I knew that Lotte had fallen for my father. Did my mother really not notice? She had fallen for him too after all. As she stood over his hospital bed in her nurse's uniform. He had slept and had not noticed her. His leg had been amputated below the knee. Just in time. Because of gangrene. Not even twenty-five he was. He had a fever, his hair stuck to his forehead, smooth and black. 'My China-man,' she says. Once, by chance, I overheard her saying to him in her soft voice: 'My little China-man'. She pats his face dry with a towel, she wets his dry lips. Tries to get him to take some tea from a beaker. He mutters in his sleep. She has to tear herself away from him and check on the other patients. She loses track of time looking at him.

True love with a disabled man. Did Lotte know how my father and mother had met? An organisation for the disabled, with him on the side of the patients, and her on the side of the carers. But the war was over. Lotte was pretty. And she wanted to be even prettier and she saw opportunities. If she heard the dragging of the prosthesis on the wood floor, she pulled her stomach in, smoothed her eyebrows quickly with spit. A love affair with a disabled man, even if he was married and had children, would nonetheless be an act of compassion and would have to be judged by different standards. Not such a great sin as with an able-bodied man who no one had ever harmed. She and he were always the first ones up in the morning. When she caught the scent of his aftershave – something my father set great store by because it marked his status in the organisation, at any rate in the morning before it faded – the anxiety would get to her and she would disappear into the pantry. Inside there were glass jars filled with water with yellow alpine butter swimming in it. She would rub a few drops of oil into her hair to smooth it, and hearing him outside, hold her breath. He would be mooching around the kitchen. Looking for coffee. Drawer open, drawer shut, container open, container shut.

She steps out of the pantry, sighs, as if she has been hunting again for something that she just can't find, like he was too at that moment, and says with a tremulous voice, half intentionally tremulous, half not, in her soft Carinthian dialect: 'Good morning, Herr Helfer, did you sleep well?' And she thinks of my mother, who is probably still sleeping, and imagines him reaching out to her half-awake under the blanket. 'I'll make you a quick cup of coffee, Herr Helfer.'

'That would be great, Lotte,' he says, 'a quick one – strong, no milk, no sugar, in the smallest cup like the Italians.'

She helps herself to some of the cook's private store of coffee beans, she knows where they are hidden – I knew too – and lets a handful trickle into the mill.

'Here, give it to me,' he says. He turns the handle.

She cuts the filter to size, so that it fits the cup, pours hot water over the coffee. She would really love to have a cup of coffee like this too. But the cook's beans have been counted, down to the nearest ten. She stands close in front of my father and hands him the cup. She nearly looks him in the eye.

'Wash under your arms,' he says – this is how I imagine my father speaking to Lotte …

He was lying on the ground in the shed, looked small. Did Lotte scream? I didn't hear her. She ran from the laboratory over to the main house, banged on all the doors. That I did hear. Not her voice.

Gretel and I were already in bed. They called the ambulance service, or the fire brigade, Gretel thinks it was the fire brigade, they came up from the valley and took our father to hospital. Aunt Irma went with him.

Gretel and I drifted like ghosts through the house. Our mother had shut herself in the bedroom. Two covers over her and the pillow wrapped around her ears. Baby Richard clutched to her breast. And not a sound. From either of them. Gretel and I hung about first in one corner then in another. Eventually we heard a car and heard Aunt Irma's voice and heard the car drive away again.

Aunt Irma called us all to the table – Gretel, our mother and me – and said: 'Vati is going to have an operation to remove part of his stomach, but he will recover, not for some time of course, but in the end, well, perhaps not completely, but more or less.'

Our mother buried her face in the pillow. She had brought it down to the dining hall with her. The cook was holding baby Richard pressed against her shoulder. The cook's husband was nodding without stopping. I nearly said to him, for everyone's sake: 'Please, Herr Fritsch, could you stop nodding!'

From now on the laboratory, the shed, seemed to me to represent the hell that the catechist rejoiced about in our religious studies class, as if it was something he was looking forward to. That's where the beetles lived. They looked scary under my father's microscope. And yet I kept wanting to look at them again.

'Shall we have a look at beetles?' he often asked me in the middle of the day.

'I'd rather not,' I said.

'Fine, then we won't,' he said.

'Well, all right,' I said.

'I'd rather not,' he said.

'Oh, come on, please!' I said.

'I don't know.'

'Please!'

'Are you sure?'

'Yes.'

'I don't know. I don't know. I don't know,' he said.

'Oh well, never mind,' I said.

'All right then,' he said.

This was our ritual. I wanted to believe it was ours alone.

The laboratory was actually only a wide table on which stood a Bunsen burner, the microscope, several small glass tubes and crucibles. He lifted me up and set me down at one end of the table.

'And now,' he said, 'recite our poem to me! Then you may look at the beetles.'

And I recited without really knowing what I was reciting:

'Flow, flow onward
Stretches many,

Spare not any
Water rushing,
Ever streaming fully downward
Toward the pool in current gushing.'

In the night the beetles crept under my covers and scrabbled around my feet, and it was no use thrashing about, and they crawled up to my neck and into my face and I ran over to my parents' bedroom and slipped into bed beside my mother.

'Go back to sleep,' she said and held me tight, so that I didn't fall out of the bed, for I wasn't lying between my parents but at the edge of the bed on her side. 'Tomorrow is another day.'

She often said this sentence. If only I could have said this sentence to her just once.

Now Aunt Irma took command. That's how she said it: 'Now I am taking command.'

She lied, out of kindness, to my sister Gretel and me. Vati had picked up the wrong glass in the semi-darkness, she said, he had been thirsty and the glass with the poison he had prepared for a chemical experiment was right next to the glass with elderberry juice and by chance looked exactly the same, and because he felt so thirsty, he had drunk it down in one go. The bad lighting in the shed was to blame, the dim lamp was to blame.

She could not fool our mother with this story. Our mother knew that her husband had wanted to take his own life. She didn't know why. Aunt Irma took a different tack with her.

The war was to blame, she said.

'We women,' she said, 'we have absolutely no idea!' That is, no idea what the men had to deal with out in the field, the things they were expected to do out there, Josef losing half his leg was the least of it. 'They can't even bring themselves to speak about the worst things, they were so bad,' that was a fact. The truth was, the worse one's experiences, the less one was able to speak about them. That had been proved, she had read about it. However, the worst things were not visible, they were locked up inside the soul, rattling away at the bars. She gave as an example her brother Lorenz, who was in Russia for a long time. 'Have you ever heard Lorenz tell any stories? You see. Me neither.' And it was exactly the same with Josef. 'We have no idea what he has had to go through.' For he could not speak about it. He was a quiet person anyway and now this. And then all of a sudden it bursts out of him. The bars break. All of a sudden. That's how Grete should think of it. He could do nothing about it. 'He's not prepared for it himself. He's sitting there in his laboratory, about to carry out a harmless experiment and then it bursts out of him. We can have no idea what he sees suddenly in front of him. What form does it take, the beast that has broken loose.' And at just this moment — with this Irma tries to comfort her sister — at that precise moment he swallowed the poison. 'One moment later and he would not have done it,' she said.

Irma knew nothing about the books that my father had 'stashed away'. She had just one aim: to stop her sister thinking that she herself was somehow to blame.

She wrote to her brothers Heinrich, Lorenz, Walter and Sepp and her older sister Kathe. She wrote: 'Come over, Grete needs us.'

Our mother just lay in bed, no longer ate anything, no longer washed herself. The cook and her husband and Lotte had made themselves scarce, probably holed up in their rooms. When the siblings who lived scattered across the country arrived, it was late morning. They climbed out of Uncle Walter's white Opel, made their way into the bedroom and stood in front of their sister's bed. Uncle Heinrich was not with them – he was needed on the farm, and anyway there would not have been enough room for him in the car. His daughter, six years older than me, had said to him he had no business getting involved with that lot up there. That strange lot up there kept themselves to themselves and should be left to look after their own affairs. Uncle Walter had told Uncle Lorenz about this, but Uncle Lorenz had said, you really don't need to tell me, I already heard about it, over the mountains, and he had pointed his finger in the girl's direction. Back over the mountains. His magic finger.

And it was Lorenz too who was the first to say anything: 'Grete,' he said, 'we'd like to see you. Crawl out from under your blanket, for goodness' sake! Show yourself! Get up! We want to talk to you!'

Gretel and I were not in the room but we were peeping through the crack in the door. Our mother did not stir. We heard only her long-drawn-out heavy breathing. What we heard and saw in front of us immediately made it clear to us both, that everything had gone to pieces. And there was nothing that could be done about it. And we had no idea what would happen to us. To the two of us. Richard will be all right, I thought, he's too small, they'll all want to look after him, the sweetie with the quiff in his hair like a cream horn pastry and his cute little belly that he stretches out in such a cute way. But what about us, Gretel and me? My knitted jacket with the fur trim had lost all significance for me, the consolation that beauty can bring to life had gone. The jacket could have belonged to anyone. Along with all my other possessions. It hung on my shoulders as if it wanted to say: I have nothing to do with this girl. Hopefully, I thought, hopefully, I will at least get to keep my sister. I pressed myself against her. And Gretel gave me a hug.

'I don't understand it either,' she whispered. And that meant a lot. That meant, you are not alone. For now, that was good enough for me.

Behind us, only now did I notice, stood Aunt Irma. I screwed up my eyes as I always did when I thought I couldn't bear the world any longer and in the distorted image she was white, her apron as white as her face. Eyes, mouth and nose blurred in whiteness. I thought, please, Gretel, do or say something else, so I know what I have to say, I'll just copy you.

Aunt Kathe sends her brothers into the kitchen, they are to wait there with Irma. She wants to speak to Grete alone. 'And, Lorenz, you tell Irma what we agreed.'

Thoughts are never what they should be, or only rarely. What I mean is, what one really thinks about in an awful moment can be so much more banal than the awful situation actually calls for. I thought: so from now, Aunt Kathe has taken command, and the fact that Aunt Irma did not enter the bedroom, where our Mutti was struggling with a despair beyond my comprehension, that was a sign, that she had relinquished her command to her older sister, voluntarily. I thought, perhaps Aunt Kathe will stay and Aunt Irma will go. Everything would not be so stressful. Aunt Kathe would tell me exactly what I had to do. And I wouldn't have to work it out by myself like with Aunt Irma, and then still get it wrong. Aunt Kathe had visited us a few times on the Tschengla, I didn't really know her. She never brought us anything, and that was fine; it made me like her. I don't know any child who enjoys saying thank you. And if you don't bring a child anything, you don't put them under any obligation to say thank you. She spoke to me as if she were speaking to an adult. I didn't have to give her a smile either. I would have found that even harder than saying thank you.

When Irma and her brothers had withdrawn into the kitchen, Aunt Kathe called us into the bedroom.

'I want you to help me,' she said. 'Yes, you two. Gretel, grab your mama under the right arm, Monika, you take the left one.'

She lifted our mother's legs. We pulled and managed to get her into a sitting position on the edge of the bed. She had closed her eyes. She said nothing. But she was still taking loud gasps of breath. I found it frightening. I had never heard anyone do that before.

'Grete,' said Aunt Kathe, 'I know you can hear me. You don't need to say anything, or nod. I will simply carry on talking. Gretel and Monika will help me. And Lorenz is here. You said yourself once that when Lorenz is around, everything turns out fine. Lorenz always makes everything turn out fine. He's cancelled everything else to be here. Sepp and Walter are here too. So come on now, up you get! Stand up! All right, stay put. Stay sitting. That will be fine. But stop gasping like that, you'll end up fainting. You don't want the children seeing that.'

Aunt Kathe dipped a cloth into the washbasin standing on the commode, put some soap onto it and washed her unresponsive sister. First her face, then her arms, then her legs, then her belly and chest. It was the first and only time, I saw our mother's breasts. Gretel, said Aunt Kathe, was to look for some clean clothes in the cupboard, stockings and a dress. We dressed our mother and she let us get on with it. Gretel brushed her hair, she could hardly pull the brush through, it was so tangled. Impatiently, she tugged at the brush, and Mutti whimpered softly. I sympathised, Gretel had always tugged at my hair like that as well and I had whimpered too. I was relieved that our mother was now whimpering and that the loud gasping that I had never heard from her before had stopped. Kathe put her shoes on for her, then she pulled her up, and we pushed her out of the bedroom and over to the kitchen where her brothers and Irma were waiting. Walter had a bottle of beer in his hand and sat on the window seat, Lorenz and Sepp were standing drinking coffee. They set out cups for their sisters, filled them with coffee and a shot of schnapps, the rowanberry schnapps, which was said to be beneficial for one's health too, good for the nerves and the stomach. Then Lorenz started speaking again, his thick, round, dark horn-rimmed glasses looked like a sort of protuberance from his skin, as if they were never removed, even at night:

'Grete, we have something to say to you. We'll be frank. This is the plan. You will come to me and my wife. Until Josef is out of hospital. Irma will look after the children. You can bring the baby with you …'

He had not yet finished speaking, before our Mutti sprang up from the bench on which we had sat her down: 'No,' she said firmly. That was all. And she began to walk around the kitchen, not unsteady at all, but cheerful and brisk, took the empty beer glass from Walter's hand and held it under running water, dried it off and put it back on the shelf, did the same with the coffee cups.

'There's some cake in the pantry,' she said. 'Would anyone like cake?'

Uncle Sepp, the youngest, good looking, like his father was said to have been, hair peeking out from under his hat, black as a raven's wing, elegant suit, narrow tie, always a cigarette between middle finger and ring finger, not between the tips of the fingers, but down by the knuckle joint, said: 'I would love a piece. Thank you, Grete.'

'It's a nut cake,' said our mother.

'Did you make it yourself?' asked Uncle Sepp. Whenever he took a drag of his cigarette, he would lay his whole hand over his mouth.

'No!' laughed our mother – she actually laughed. 'I can't make cakes! None of us can make cakes.'

'I can make a cake,' said Irma.

'One like this?'

'If I put my mind to it.'

'But not one like this.'

'But one that's just as good. Like my rhubarb cake.'

Mutti turned to me, it would have to be me: 'Monika, tell us truthfully! Do you like Aunt Irma's rhubarb cake? Be absolutely honest now!'

And then finally, finally, she wept. No loud, scary gasping. But a quite normal weeping. The kind we are familiar with. From our own selves and from others. We were all relieved.

Aunt Kathe did not stay and our mother did not move in with Uncle Lorenz and his wife. Aunt Irma took command once more. She made an effort. Tried to be gentle. And indeed she was towards her sister, not so much towards Gretel and me. She never forgave me that I was the one our mother had asked if I liked her rhubarb cake. I had said, yes, I like it. But that counted for nothing. Mutti had asked *me*, she wanted to hear that I didn't like it. If she had wanted a different answer, she would have asked someone else.

One day we walked down the mountain and caught the bus to the hospital to visit our father. Lotte came too. Maybe the cook as well. Not our mother.

He lay in bed on his side, very thin he was, his face gaunt and pale, his hair long and unwashed. His prosthesis was leaning against the bedside table. We girls stood beside the bed, feeling shy, as if he were a stranger. He beckoned us over to him.

'Would you like a dessert?' he asked.

I looked over to Gretel.

'We don't know what that is,' she said.

'Of course you know,' he said. 'We're in the hotel business, are we not? I'm a hotel manager.'

Gretel looked over at me, I shrugged my shoulders slightly.

'We don't know exactly what that is,' she said.

'Not exactly?' asked my father. 'So you do have a bit of an idea?'

We nodded. I did too, although I didn't have even a bit of an idea.

'Something to do with hotels?' asked Gretel.

'A dessert,' he said, 'is a pudding. Would you like one? It's mostly yellow with a blob of red in the middle.'

I looked over to Aunt Irma. I saw she was thinking of the rhubarb cake and so I said: 'I'd like a pudding.'

'I can chase one up for you,' he said. He pressed the button on the bell that hung above him. One of the sisters appeared and, as if she were a waitress, he ordered two puddings and two Sinalco drinks.

While we were in the middle of eating and drinking, Aunt Irma said: 'Your Vati wants to give you some important news.'

Until then no one had ever 'given me important news'. I was told things but not given important news about them. I was frightened and I saw that Gretel was frightened too. The effect on her, an automatic reaction really, was that she shifted a step closer to me.

To protect me or to be protected by me, she did not know herself.

'So, Josef!' insisted Aunt Irma.

No, I don't think Lotte and the cook were there. Or they left earlier. That's possible. Perhaps they wanted to do some shopping in the town. When I look back – and I can remember this moment very clearly, I could almost describe what the blanket lying over my father looked like; he had tucked it between his legs but in a way that only his good leg was on view – Lotte and the cook are not there, it's just my sister Gretel, our Aunt Irma and me, standing around the bed.

Aunt Irma once more: 'So, Josef! Tell them, Josef! That's why we came.'

That our Mutti is pregnant. That was the important news. That we are going to have a new brother or sister. I thought: now, when Richard is still a babe in arms?

As we were saying goodbye to our father, something happened that Gretel and I still talk about today. The door to the hospital room opened and a very fat man burst in, looked around, stammered something about having got the doors mixed up, made a tutting sound, was about to go again, when his gaze fell upon our father.

'Hey!' he exclaimed. 'Is that you, Josef? Of course it's you! Hey, my goodness, you're still in the land of the living!'

And Aunt Irma, tart as only she could be: 'Has anyone indicated the contrary?'

'Not at all,' murmured the fat guy.

'Why do you say something like that then? In front of the children? This is their father lying here!'

'It's just a turn of phrase,' the man backtracked, stammering. 'I didn't mean to offend.' And to our father: 'You know, don't you, Josef, I didn't mean to offend. It's just something people say, when they haven't seen someone for a long time: hey, hello, you're still in the land of the living. I didn't know that you were in such a bad way.'

Our father burst out laughing at this. It was that spontaneous laughter that we so rarely heard. The same laughter as later in the gay bar in Berlin that my sister Renate had taken us to – Renate, who, as we had just been informed, was at that time swimming in our mother's belly. No one knew then whether it would be a boy or a girl. Gretel and I wanted a girl. A little sister. On the last page of our school note-book, we wrote down a list of the girls' names we would give our new sister, if we were her mother.

Our father remained in hospital a lot longer – one year. Why so long? Was there some other reason? His wife gave birth to a girl. She named her Renate – that was not one of the names on our list. A home birth. The midwife took care of our mother, did not want to leave her side until everything was properly sorted out. She gave Gretel and me instructions and we managed the housekeeping well. Aunt Irma was jealous. Jealous also because our mother was getting better. The thing was: Irma used to be a member of the family, the same as everyone else, then she had taken charge, and for her that meant she had gone up a step. When our mother said to her: 'You don't have to worry about me any more, Irma, I can manage now,' it sounded to her as if she had said: 'Irma, we don't need you now.' My mother meant to say however: now you can go back to how things were before. Aunt Irma took her unhappiness out on me. She found fault with me even more than before. Our brother, Richard, on the other hand, was cosseted by her. Anyone visiting, any stranger, would have thought Irma was the mother of the little boy. If I am not mistaken, one of the disabled men once hinted something to that effect. Gretel says today I'm just imagining that. Yes, I'm just imagining hearing him say to Aunt Irma: 'You have such a lovely little boy.' And I am just imagining hearing her answer: 'He is, isn't he.'

To Gretel and me, Renate seemed very tiny. But she was beautiful. Always a bit rosy. We loved watching her most when she kicked her little legs, it made us laugh each time. Gretel and I took turns cuddling her, Gretel for a bit, then me for a bit, we checked on the clock in the dining hall, each of us exactly five minutes.

Our mother wrapped Renate in sheets and blankets and together with Lotte went down the mountain and into town to visit our father in hospital. It was too dangerous for our mother to carry the baby, said Lotte, and took the bundle from her. What if she stumbled! She walked unsteadily in her small, chamois leather shoes. There was a bit of colour in our father's face. Lotte confirmed this. And he was now able to walk around the hospital for half an hour. His suit hung off him, he had lost so much weight. He was allowed to consume only dairy products. His favourite was sour milk, in which he soaked slices of black bread until they had practically dissolved, and then he spooned it up.

And then one day Vati was back with us again. But it was as if Gretel and I were invisible, little Richard, too, who had now started walking and constantly toddled along behind Gretel and me, always laughing, never crying. Vati showed no interest even in baby Renate. We were all invisible to him. Our mother was the only one who meant something to him. Not something, everything. The two of them sat on the terrace as if they were summer visitors. And we served them hot chocolate and bread and ham. He would read aloud to her. *Kristin Lavransdatter*. We were not invited to come and listen. They were a couple in love. Mutti's head was permanently glued to his shoulder. Aunt Irma was in charge of setting the rules, she took control again. And occasionally she even smiled at me.

Everything was all right.

In an almost terrible way, everything had turned out all right. No one had actually given a damn about the books. Even if our father had 'stashed away' all of the books, no one would have cared, no one would have called him to account. They would probably even have been grateful to him. That he had organised their disposal. In advance. This man thinks ahead, he knows what needs to be done, he doesn't wait to be told what to do, that's the kind of man who's needed, that's the kind of man the country needs. He had taken the poison needlessly. He had atoned. But for something no one saw as needing atonement. Such fear! Wanting to die because of an all-consuming fear! So much anguish! Just like the Seven Swabians! They prepare themselves for the worst, and then the worst turns out to be a hare!

Yes, everything turned out all right – in a terrible way everything turned out all right.

I have never set foot in the forest again. I don't even know if my father ever recovered the buried books. I have inherited a part of his library, another part went to Renate and another to Gretel. The Kant volumes, the copy of *Des Knaben Wunderhorn* and the fine edition of *Don Quixote* were not there. When many years ago my husband and I drove our VW bus up to the Tschengla, because I wanted to show him where I had grown up, I contemplated searching for the spot. I looked up to the edge of the forest, everything was exactly the same as back then. I didn't do it. The fallen tree would almost certainly not have been left lying. This was not virgin forest. It would have attracted bark beetle. Loggers would have sawed it up and transported it away. Perhaps they found the packages. And shared the books out amongst themselves. Or the treasure is still lying there. That's what a treasure should be, something that remains hidden.

I have still not said anything at all about our school! The truth is: I remember almost nothing. I remember the walk to and from school. That Gretel always dawdled so much. She stopped at every worm. And she never dared to do anything. She was a stroller, not an adventurer. Even when we were in a hurry, she would straggle behind. I was always in a hurry. She never was. Like our father. When he went walking, no matter where, it always looked as if he had no goal in mind. As if he were just out for a stroll. A *flâneur*, one might have said, had he been one of those he had always wanted to be, a city dweller.

Once he said to me: 'When you're walking, you think about sitting, when you're sitting, you think about lying down, when you lie down, you think about walking. Nothing will come of that.'

'Nothing will come of what?' I asked. I was a bit older by then, had already read Karl Jaspers. And had already met Karl Jaspers in person. 'Do you want to argue with me about nothingness?'

Another time my brother, Richard, said the same thing to me. That I thought about sitting when walking, about lying down when sitting and so on.

'What about you?' I said.

'Me,' he said, 'when I'm walking, I think about lying down, when I'm sitting or standing, I think about lying down, and when flying, I think about lying down too. I always think about lying down.'

No, I remember nothing about primary school. Only about the walk to and from school. I considered school to be time stolen from me.

It was a winter's day. When we left the school building, the sun was still shining, bitterly cold, not a cloud. There was so much snow lying that the path up over the mountain was like a channel cut into the ground, to the right and to the left were walls of snow. Every sound was muffled. Now and then we saw ravens flying across the strip of sky. Gretel was dawdling again, took off her gloves, dug grooves with her fingers into the smooth wall of snow. Then a wind got up.

I said: 'That's the two-faced wind.'

That was a name that we had invented. Two-faced, because it made a pretence of being gentle, even slightly warm, like a Foehn wind, though the Foehn was itself two-faced, behaving as if spring had arrived.

But this two-faced wind was no Foehn. It seduced one into folly.

Our folly was that we wanted to leave the path. That is, I wanted to. I wanted us to do the last stretch, the steepest part, battling through the deep snow.

'But it's over our heads!' protested Gretel.

To my mind that was exactly what would make it fun. I said we should dig a tunnel, a secret passage; and that we would have snow above us and on either side, just glittering snow, sparkling in the sunlight above the tunnel, although in actual fact the sun was no longer shining. She didn't want to go along with this, said Gretel. I said, well, don't then, I'll just go by myself. Because I could rely on the fact that in the end she would come with me.

We had already gone quite a way – it wasn't really that hard, the snow was as light as a feather quilt and not all that deep on the steep part of the slope – when the sky darkened and very quickly the two-faced wind turned into a storm. We dug faster, me at the front; there were only a few metres to go till we reached the next bend, we didn't want to turn back. The storm was whirling up the snow, while at the same time fresh snow had started to fall.

Gretel was in tears behind me. I slipped and fell on my knee, the ground underneath the snow was frozen hard. I had a hole in my woollen stockings, I was bleeding, the snow had worked its way into my stockings and into my shoes. Soon the snow covered our heads, then the ceiling caved in and snow fell down the back of our necks. A tree crashed down. Then a second one, not far from us. There was a creaking and a groaning, as if old men were taking up arms. But huge old men.

Gretel was praying. We reached the path but at the little wayside shrine, I fell again and this time I really hurt myself – there was something wrong with my ankle, I could no longer put any weight on it. Gretel dragged me to her side, I put my arm around her.

'Stop crying!' I said. I said it to stop myself from weeping too. My face was smeared with snot, our hair wet, I could no longer feel my legs because of the cold. Melting snow ran down my back. I wet my pants, which took me by surprise, for I had not expected to feel so afraid.

'Help!' called Gretel.

'Help!' we shouted. 'Help!'

We heard a car. Some people picked us up. They took off my shoes to see what was wrong with my ankle. They had woollen socks with them. They were so big that the heels reached up to my calves.

Back at home, no one was interested in listening to our story. For it was on that very day that a more important matter had come to light. Our mother was wearing dark sunglasses ...

Chaos on the computer screen.

I had created a folder with the title: 'Mutti'.

Then saved all documents there.

It turned out that I had two identical documents. I had absent-mindedly given them both the same title.

The computer asked me: 'Do you want to replace the file?'

I clicked: 'Yes.'

And the correct one was gone.

That's what happens, I thought to myself, when I want to talk about our Mutti. She is like a bird flitting past. Hardly has she arrived before she disappears again.

I see her standing by the kitchen window, her hand resting on the sill; nearby a coal tit hops from one grain to another, the smallest member of this family, it pecks from our Mutti's hand, the blackbird also pecks from her hand, but not the sparrow, it stands and watches. She moves her hand away, then it takes what is lying on the sill and flutters around.

I ask her: 'Are you going to feed the deer again today? Can I come with you today? They always run away from me. You can tell them, I'm with you.'

'First thing tomorrow morning,' she says, 'it's too late now for today.'

I go to the cellar and fetch a head of cabbage, pick off the leaves and cut them into strips.

'So that's for the deer,' I say. 'Can I come with you tomorrow?'

'I'll think about it,' says my mother.

'Please say yes,' I say.

The more important matter that came to light that day was: our mother had cancer.

The days grew dark, Mutti was soon lying in hospital and we sensed that she would never recover. We had that feeling because everything changed. When our father had been in hospital, everything had not changed. But now we had to move out of the Convalescent Home for War-wounded. We were taken first to one place, then to another: strange faces, strange beds. No Richard, no Renate. Just Gretel and me. Richard was with Aunt Irma. But where was Renate? No one told us what was really going on. I don't remember what our father was doing. He is missing from the images in my head. He was always at the hospital, Gretel tells me. Because it wasn't very busy in the hospital, they had put our Mutti in a single room and moved a bed in there for our father. Not because they were important people, of course, that was not the case. But because of the exceptional plight of this man.

'Are those your words?' I ask.

'No,' says Gretel. 'That's what they said. I was told that's what they said.'

'"Exceptional plight of this man"?'

'Correct.'

'One hundred per cent correct?' I ask.

'With a memory, what does one hundred per cent look like,' she says.

'Perhaps you just want your own version,' I say.

'I don't think up words like that,' she says. 'Those are the sort of words that *you* think up.'

'If that's really how it was …' I say.

'Why would it not have been!' She gets annoyed. As if I were implying the contrary. But the contrary could only hold true, had there been less love between our parents than there actually was.

'I have no idea,' I say.

Paradise had come to an end! We children were divided up. Richard went to Aunt Irma. She in the meantime had a boyfriend. Whom she soon married, after just a month. A huge man. A colossus. We could hear him approaching a good two minutes before he entered the house, his voice was so loud. It boomed through the surrounding countryside. Like the voice of Archangel Michael with his sword. A blind colossus. From now on: our Uncle Pirmin. Blind, but not blinded in the war. He underwent training as a masseur and developed his own technique, with which he put hopeless cases back on their feet – one of them would become my husband in the distant future. Whenever he entered the dining hall, he would bang his head against the door lintel. A huge head. The whole house boomed and cracked. The blind Samson who brings the palace crashing down.

This was his constant refrain: 'It's only fair that God has taken away my vision. He has given me far too much of everything else.'

Our brother, Richard, went to them. That went without saying. Aunt Irma had always acted anyway as if he were hers.

And little Renate and Gretel and me? Aunt Kathe took us in. We went to Bregenz. To the *Südtirolersiedlung*, the South Tyrolean Settlement, a housing development built during the Second World War for refugees. We moved into the three-bedroom flat where five people were already living.

'Just till your mother gets better,' said Aunt Kathe. She did not even attempt to believe in this herself.

There was this feeling of having been caught doing something wrong. Our Mutti had now died and I stood at the graveside and thought to myself: I just hope no one sees me. I was aware however that my school class was gathered somewhere in front of the bushes near the cemetery wall. I was the new girl, hardly arrived, and her mother dies. The funeral was embarrassing for me. To our classmates we were a bit of a nuisance, and a bit weird. And now they had to come to the cemetery, teacher's orders. I stood close to Gretel, who was snuffling, the corners of her mouth turned down. In front of us, between us, was Richard, we held him tight. He turned round and stamped about in his small, tight summer shoes, though it was already November, but he did not dare make a sound. He was scared of the hole. How can a four-year-old comprehend the idea of a person,

alive or dead, being stuffed into a hole? Beside me
Aunt Irma kept bending over to check on him. Then
he looked over at her, and Gretel and I pressed him
closer to us, to make it clear to everyone else that
he belonged to us. He was wearing the little knitted
coat with a hood that our Mutti had bought for him
and that had been far too big for him at the time.
Now it fitted him. If she had only known that he
would wear it for the first time at her funeral. I had
no idea where little Renate was. In someone's arms
further back. It was unlikely that we could be kept
together. That's what I was thinking. Perhaps one of
us will be left by the wayside. No one cares enough
about us. They'll ask: who's going to have her? Who's
going to have him? And they'll say: it doesn't really
matter, does it? As long as she has somewhere to lay
her head and gets something to eat and behaves at
school, they'll find each other again eventually in the
future. They're no trouble. That would be a different
matter entirely. It was November and the weather was
unfunny, as our father used to call weather like this,
foggy, and I thought to myself: if only this was all
over, everyone being so childish, saying that we will
never see our Mutti again, really and truly never
again. To believe that seemed childish to me. Like
when someone pretended to be a ghost. A damp
cold permeated up from below. I pressed my legs
together so that I did not wet my pants again.
That was the last thing I needed. I was particularly

embarrassed by the voice of Aunt Irma's husband. As the Lord's Prayer was being said, it sounded like he was the only one praying and the others were just mumbling softly in the background, even the crows flew off. The fact that he had such large hands could make me blush too. That when praying he extended his hands way out in front; of course he couldn't see what that looked like, he was blind, but all the same. As if everything revolved around him. Now and forever more, people will think of him as one of us, I thought. I was ashamed that the girls in my class could all see how horrible the bow in my hair looked. And how poor we were. Dressed so shabbily. To be without a mother is to be without a sense of self-worth. She couldn't cook but she gave us a sense of self-worth. Of course, then I did not know the meaning of this phrase, but today I do. Everyone knows: Gretel and I are placed with poor people, we were even poorer than the poor, the poorest of the poor were our benefactors. They were sent off to visit us, our school friends, turning up one after the other at the South Tyrolean Settlement, to offer their condolences. Aunt Kathe dealt with them all at the door, she did not let any of them come in. She did not even take off her apron. The idea had occurred to one of the teachers and he had organised it. Just a small gesture, he'd thought to himself. 'Go and say to Gretel and Monika that you're sorry to hear that their mama has died. Off you go now!' Monika and

Gretel have only one grey pleated skirt, one green blouse, one blue pleated skirt and one white blouse each. The coffin chosen was one made of cardboard. That was the bottom of the range. The graveside address by the cable car owner was all about his cable car. Why had he been the one to speak? Had no one else been available? Up on the Tschengla, after the war, an idyllic island had been created, he said, offering many people so many wonderful experiences. I was half expecting him to announce that the Convalescent Home for War-wounded, now that we had moved out, was finally going to be turned into a hotel, or already had been, and that all the mourners were heartily invited to travel up in the cable car, where bread and *Wurst* would be served free of charge.

I wanted to sink into the ground and felt that if I made an immense effort, I could do it. I imagined that there was a cable linked to each of my eyes and that all I had to do was concentrate, fix my eyes on the ground, hold my breath, take hold of each eye and pull. This image came into my mind as the cable car owner was shaking my hand and muttering something. I remembered that he had hit his dimwit son on the hands, hard enough to make them bleed, so that he would not have to sit the test at school, and no one would see what a dimwit he was. And that the son was proud of having such a smart father. The sound of sobbing beside me and in front of me and behind me scraped like a rasp over my back and my sides.

I was eleven.

Then in the evening we sat in the kitchen at Aunt Kathe's in the South Tyrolean Settlement – Uncle Lorenz, Uncle Walter and Uncle Sepp, side by side on the flowery sofa, the legs of which had already broken off twice since we moved in here, because too many people had sat on it. Aunt Irma was standing, Aunt Kathe was standing, and squatting on the stool was her husband, who I had still not got used to over the last six months, a man of just skin and bones, who nourished himself solely on beer. Everyone was silent, as if they had been switched off. So many people! So little space! Aunt Kathe had three children of her own, two boys around our age and a girl a bit older. They used to quake in front of their skinny father. Then there was Gretel, Richard and me, and little Renate, who was always sitting on a different lap somewhere, just watching, never crying, always just watching with her big round cherry eyes. And in the middle like the mast on a pirate ship was Uncle Pirmin, the blind giant, thundering his words of advice into the kitchen every few minutes. I am amazed that there was any air left at all with so many mouths sharing it. I don't hold it against anyone if they get confused by so many people. I found it confusing too.

Then Uncle Sepp broke the silence, saying: 'By the way, where's Josef?'

'How should I know!' boomed Uncle Pirmin. 'Can't help! Look at me! Standing right here.'

'No one's criticising you for being blind,' said Aunt Irma.

'Where is he?' asked Uncle Sepp once again. One thing I forgot to describe: all the men were smoking, the blind man's head high above us disappeared in a blue haze.

'Monika, Gretel!' he called down to us. 'Don't you know where your father is? Shouldn't it be your job to know where he is at a time like this?'

'Leave the two of them in peace,' said Aunt Irma.

No one had noticed until now that our father was not there, not until now, a good two hours had passed since the funeral, and only now does anyone notice that the husband of the deceased is not here!

'When we were receiving condolences,' said Irma, 'he was definitely still there, he was accepting a handshake from everyone.'

'You put that very nicely, Irma!' roared Pirmin. 'Accepting a handshake from everyone! That's my Irma!'

'Just be quiet for half an hour for once,' said Aunt Irma – and at that point both disappear from my memories of that afternoon.

Aunt Kathe said: 'No one ever gets lost.' I often used to hear her say this later on. I like this expression and if I imagine it being said in her voice, it comforts me even today. Sometimes when something gives me a feeling of tightness in my chest, I say the sentence softly to myself and try to imitate Aunt Kathe's voice.

What Uncle Lorenz and Uncle Walter contributed, I cannot remember. Gretel says that back then she could not have distinguished one from the other with any certainty – Uncle Walter, the tall one, slim with red hair and a pockmarked face, who always had a joke at the ready, even when everyone around him was 'grizzling', that's what we say for 'crying' in these parts, and Uncle Lorenz about whom we knew many stories, so many that we almost preferred to believe that he did not really exist. She used to be scared of both of them, says Gretel. She was scared of all the men in the family – except for our Vati and a bit less so of our elegant Uncle Sepp, whom we knew a bit better, as he had a motorbike and often drove up to see us, always a surprise visit. He was our mother's favourite brother.

'Josef? He can't have disappeared from the face of the earth,' said Aunt Irma.

And I was thinking: but what if he has?

We had not been in Bregenz very long and did not know our way around. Whether Vati knew his way around, we had no idea.

Then the big search began. Uncle Lorenz, Uncle Walter and Uncle Sepp spread out, with no idea of course where they should look for their brother-in-law, it would have been pure chance had they come across him in the street or anywhere else. First of all, they sent Sepp out to check in the cemetery, and if he were to find him there, that is, at the grave – 'then leave him be!'

But he was not at the cemetery. 'So let's spread out!'

When the brothers were outside, Aunt Kathe said to her husband: 'Aren't you going to go?'

The man who we were supposed to call Uncle Theo said: 'I don't even know what he looks like.'

'You don't know what my brother-in-law looks like?'

'I'm not quite sure.'

'How sure then?'

'Not sure enough.'

'Then sit yourself down and get your grey matter working, and when you remember what he looks like, go and help my brothers look for him!'

That's what he did. He sat down at the kitchen table, stared straight ahead, his cheek muscles twitched, you could see each one of them under his taut skin, his mouth a lipless gash, a cigarette on the left-hand side. After a few minutes he stood up, grinned through his brown molars on the right and said: 'Just for you, Kathe, but only for you.'

And went off. We saw him through the window, standing down in the street and lighting up his next cigarette, moving his lower jaw as if he were chewing the filter. He smoked cigarettes from Switzerland.

That was where he worked. Everything in Switzerland was better than here. Even the sugar was sweeter. The noodles were more yellow. The chocolate, well, there was just no comparison. Same with soup seasoning, no comparison. The cigarettes with their gold filters looked chic. When we were still living up on the Tschengla, we children knew nothing of this blessed country. Whoever had found a job there could boast without a qualm.

In the end, Uncle Sepp found our father in Mehrerauer Wood down by the lake. Rain was dripping through the trees, he saw him walking along slowly – his hair wet, the coat over his shoulders drenched with rain, his hands dug into his pockets. Uncle Sepp was very gentle with him. He took his arm and led him to Aunt Kathe's apartment. Both of them good-looking, small, sensitive men. Those who have assumed a mask recognise one another. No one else can read their faces, but between mask wearers there is a mutual awareness. Uncle Sepp would have liked to have found some words of consolation, but everything seemed inadequate, so he just clasped his brother-in-law's arm to his side and they walked on in silence. They left the path and made their way through the undergrowth in the woods, had to duck down and climb over fallen debris. It seemed the paths were not made for them, but could nevertheless lead them out of their pain.

These two men were the ones who loved our mother the most.

Mutti had told us that in the bitter winter of 1931 when she was a schoolgirl, and her parents were no longer alive, Sepp had waited for her in front of the school. A lad approached him, a tall boy who'd already left school, and asked him: 'Are you waiting for the cuckoo?' Uncle Sepp was a shy person all his life, as a child, he'd always taken care of his appearance, so he washed himself every day, and it was important to him that the things he wore were more or less matching. 'What do you mean, cuckoo?' he asked in his soft voice. 'Who are you calling a cuckoo?' The tall lad explained it to him. That he meant Grete. That she had been planted in the Bagage family nest. Just like a cuckoo puts its egg in the nest of another bird and then out from the egg pops a cuckoo and not a magpie. The same old story again. The reason why the priest had taken down the crucifix at my family's house. Because my grandmother, the beautiful Maria, was said to be a whore, who got involved with other men while her own husband was fighting for emperor and fatherland. Sepp said nothing. He had, and this was told to me not by my mother, but by Aunt Kathe, when she was almost one hundred, he had not immediately understood exactly what an insult this was. Not even when Grete came out of school and ran up to him, and the older lad said: 'Here she comes, your cuckoo.'

'Don't let him get to you,' said Grete to Sepp, whose face didn't give anything away, it never did, a face like a beautiful mask. But Grete knew him and she said once again: 'Don't get worked up about it! It doesn't matter. Let him say what he likes!' But he did get worked up about it, it did matter to him, and he didn't want this lad to say such things ever again, especially this boy. He knew the story of his brother Lorenz, who had defended his mother against the mayor, when he had tried to force himself on her. And he thought, now it was up to him to defend his sister. Secretly he fetched the shotgun from the house, draped his jacket over it and made his way the very same day down into the village, he knew where the older boy lived. So he went down the road, first on the rough rubble track that led to the last house before the mountain, that is, their own house, then on along the fine gravel road into the village. Now he no longer concealed the gun. It was pure chance, so says my sister Gretel, divine providence, that a man who was walking along the road saw the nine-year-old with his set face and with the shotgun in both hands heading towards the village at a fast pace; he knew the boy, he was one of the Bagage, you knew what to expect from that lot. The man ran as fast as he could up to the house and when he got as far as the water trough, called up to Lorenz, and Lorenz ran after his brother and caught him just as he was standing in front of the house in which the lad lived. What did he want with the gun? 'The same as you,' Uncle Sepp is supposed to have replied. And everyone in our family was and remains convinced that he would have shot the lad who insulted his sister Grete, if Lorenz had not prevented him.

And because Grete was always my Uncle Sepp's favourite sister, he had made it his business to keep a watchful eye on my father too.

When he found him in Mehrerauer Wood – this is how I like to imagine the conversation went – he said: 'Josef, you've never ridden a motorbike before, have you?'

And Vati would answer: 'I'd have liked to, but no, I haven't.'

Uncle Sepp: 'I'll pick you up on Sunday on my Puch 250.'

'The black one?'

'Yes, that's the one. Two-seater.'

'What a great machine.'

'I'll polish it up.'

'And where are we going to go?'

'Across to Germany perhaps. Round Lake Constance. A rest stop in Meersburg. Have a good meal. Then on to Konstanz and into Switzerland and back here.'

'Or up to Cologne?'

'You can't do that in one day. What do you want to go to Cologne for anyway, Josef?'

'Or to Hamburg.'

'And then onto a ship?'

'Cologne, Hamburg, Frankfurt, Berlin. Or Ulm. Or Mannheim.'

'How about Munich, Josef? Leave early in the morning and then have some *Weisswurst* sausages in Munich, ride back in the afternoon and be home by the evening. That's doable.'

'Or Zurich.'

'Even better. Yes, Josef! Zurich airport!'

'That would be fun. I've never been on a plane.'

'Me neither. We can watch other people flying off. Then a Zurich veal casserole for lunch and come back in the afternoon.'

'I'll look forward to it, Sepp.'

'Me too, Josef!'

Our Vati loved to talk about cities all over the world. He liked to say their names aloud. Rangoon. Surabaya. Lisbon. Rio de Janeiro. Later, when he had remarried, and we were sitting having dinner together, he sometimes tested us on capital cities. We girls, Gretel and I, always lost. Renate knew a lot, Richard knew them all. Venezuela? Caracas. Angola? Luanda. Florida? Tallahassee. In spite of everything, those were lovely evenings. They were not paradise, that was up at 1,220 metres above sea level, now out of our reach.

Hamburg was our father's favourite city. He had been there once. To pick up Renate. She was sixteen and had run away from home. Because she had fallen in love with a hippy. Then Interpol contacted us. His daughter had been caught shoplifting – she had stolen a sleeping bag. Someone needed to come and get her. Our father rushed off and caught the train to Hamburg and got Renate released. And he didn't give her a hard time, quite the opposite, he strolled with her from the young offenders' prison to the Dom funfair, and they tried out all the rides, he got in beside her for the ghost train, and he let her shoot for a teddy bear. And then they visited the harbour and wandered through St Pauli slurping ice cream. Not a word about the shoplifting, not a word about her running away.

Yes, Uncle Sepp had resolved not to let his brother-in-law out of his sight, and at that given moment he wanted to show him proof of his friend-ship. That was to be more than just talk. He couldn't play chess as well as Lorenz, and he didn't have as much to say about the universe as his brother nor about history either – he couldn't care less what Napoleon had got up to – but with him one could have a comfortable silence. Our father liked to have someone around him who knew how to be silent.

Aunt Kathe brought our father some dry clothes and said she wanted to prepare some mulled wine now, they all deserved it. She sent one of her sons over to the local tavern, Gasthaus zum Sternen, to fetch a two-litre bottle of red. He was to get them to put it on account.

We saw our father only briefly in the borrowed clothes, a beige jacket with a zip that a buddy of Uncle Theo had once left behind. After that we did not see our Vati again for a long time. It was as if a piece of time had been cut out of my life. The cruel scissors left very little behind. So little, it was in danger of being forgotten …

Aunt Kathe's apartment consisted of the parents' bedroom, the children's bedroom, the living room and the kitchen, and then there was a tiny bathroom with a sitting bathtub, a washbasin and the toilet – over it a very small window that was hard to open, you had to climb onto the toilet bowl, and then snake your hand through the cleaning products on the window ledge. I missed our toilet on the Tschengla, with its window of frosted glass, a normal, large window, and when you opened it you could see the birch tree in front of the house, and no one rattled the door handle when I had a 'session', as our father used to call it, for there was a second bathroom. Until our arrival in the South Tyrolean Settlement, the living room was only used at Christmas, for the Christmas tree and the exchanging of gifts, they didn't go in for singing. Aunt Kathe served up the Christmas meal back in the kitchen, it did not differ much from the Sunday

menu for the rest of the year: soup, meat, vegetables and potatoes, rice or noodles. I didn't like rice
because when I saw it freshly cooked, I could already
anticipate its reappearance tomorrow and the day
after added to a soup. We stayed in the kitchen the
whole day, all of us – our cousins, a girl and two boys,
the three of us, Aunt Kathe and Uncle Theo, and not
infrequently Uncle Walter and Uncle Sepp. Our girl
cousin slept on the sofa in the kitchen, but if she
got tired before the end of the evening, she would
creep into her parents' bed, and then be woken in the
night and have to totter back into the kitchen. She
claimed that it didn't bother her in the least, out of
kindness to us, that was what she claimed. She didn't
want us to feel guilty. Though we were the ones who
had upset everything. Where did she sleep before we
moved in? Surely not in the living room? That was
never discussed.

My sisters, Renate and Gretel, and I, we slept in the
living room; Gretel, the oldest, on the sofa, Renate
and me on the floor, on mattresses that I had to lift up
in the morning and lean against the sideboard to air.
We were privileged. It's true it was cold in the living
room, but the air was fresh. In the kitchen it was
almost unbearable. Uncle Theo was a chain-smoker
and, not infrequently, Uncle Sepp and Uncle Walter
came to visit – Uncle Lorenz not so often – and
they too all lit up one cigarette from another. The
kitchen was no more than four metres long by four

metres wide, after just half an hour the wall opposite was barely visible. During the day, we were not allowed to go into the living room. The reason for this was something else that was never discussed. We were only allowed to enter to get something urgent from our suitcase, and then, quick march, straight out again. By order of Aunt Kathe. I am guessing that she did not want her own children to get jealous of us: why are they allowed to do what we are only allowed to do at Christmas? Her husband did not get involved. He sat in the kitchen and drank beer – on his right the full bottles, on his left the empties – and gazed out over the ashtray in front of him, into space. I used to wonder if he ever thought about anything at all. He never said a word. Except when someone opened their 'gob' when he was listening to the news on the radio, which he did at the top of every hour, then he let rip.

Sometimes there were so many people in the kitchen you couldn't turn around. Uncle Walter liked to bring a girlfriend over, rarely his wife. Aunt Kathe seldom liked any of these girlfriends, most were fat and took up twice as much space, but she was friendly, admittedly in her own way; only those who knew her well could tell if she liked someone or not.

On the Tschengla, out of season, we'd had all twenty rooms of the Convalescent Home just to ourselves. If Gretel and I had wanted, we could have slept one night here, one night there. No one would have stopped us. There was a black-framed inset in the panel of the door to each room, with a lifelike oil painting of an alpine plant on it. Underneath was its name – 'Alpine Rose room', 'Blue Gentian room', 'Yellow Gentian room', 'Edelweiss room', 'Cuckoo Flower room' and so on. Gretel and I loved acting out fairy tales, 'Snow White' for example; the queen's castle in which the mirror hung was in the Alpine Rose room, where there really was a full-length mirror leaning against the wall, the dwarves' house was in the 'Umbrella Pine Tree room' and Snow White's coffin stood in the 'Turk's Cap Lily room'. Gretel lay there on the bed with hands crossed, for she was Snow White and I, the evil queen. Or we played hide and seek with Mutti, Lotte and the cook and it was no easy task to find us in that sprawling house. Where was there to hide in Aunt Kathe's kitchen? Only behind our own closed eyelids.

I liked Aunt Kathe. I was a bit afraid of her, but I did not feel anxious if I found myself on my own with her. I think I was scared of everyone in the family back then, not like Gretel, who was only scared of the men, at any rate in our early days in the South Tyrolean Settlement. Especially the older boy cousin, he enjoyed winding us up, hiding our things or spitting in our soup, not metaphorically but literally. He had a poor relationship with his father. I almost felt sorry for him. He could never do anything right.

Whatever his father said to him always had an exclamation mark at the end. Nothing but commands. The leather belt was kept handy on the kitchen sideboard. To be used for beatings. This son was the only one who was beaten. When his father used the strap, Aunt Kathe left the kitchen. Once he hit with the buckle. Then she intervened. I heard what her son said to her later in the corridor, the blood running from his ear across his neck and his shoulders to his upper arm: 'When I'm sixteen, I'm going to hit back.' I don't know if he did. I don't know what became of him. I don't know what became of his younger brother either.

Our girl cousin was different, she made an effort to be kind to us. When she came back home with cakes or sweets, she would give them to us, she didn't keep any for herself. But I couldn't help feeling that we were a nuisance for her too. And I reckoned that one day her patience would run out. And then what? All of them, I thought, are waiting for the moment when we finally get out of their hair. I am not at all resentful of this when I remember it today, and even then I was not resentful towards them. I myself felt that we were imposing on them. No, I thought, if it were my home, I would not be able to tolerate having people like us coming to live there. Our cousin was sympathetic and kind-hearted, she didn't think like that, she gave us the sweets gladly. She was four years older than me and when she was seventeen, she was already contemplating moving out and getting married. She had a boyfriend, a very attractive Italian with an attractive name. She will marry him, and they will be happy, he will die before her.

Aunt Kathe had a set idea of how everything should be. This goes like this, and that goes that way, and the third one goes so. Every time her voice took on that particular resolute tone, she took a weight off my shoulders. She organised everything. Shoe cleaning, airing clothes, sweeping out, scrubbing floors, washing up and drying after meals, collecting apples in Dr Schallerbach's garden on the far side of the South Tyrolean Settlement – 'They'll only rot otherwise, but watch you don't get caught, and if you do, don't let on who you are!' She decreed who was to do their homework at the kitchen table and when; who was to have a bath on Saturday and who they would share the water with; which of us girls could do the ironing and who was to fold and so on. Everyone was assigned tasks, except for her husband, she did not expect anything from him. She did not give any praise if I had done everything correctly, but she would give me a look, and grin her signature grin and that counted for a lot. Gretel and I knew that we were here because Aunt Kathe had made the decision, because Aunt Kathe was one of the Bagage clan and the Bagage never leave their own in the lurch. She was still grieving for her dead sister. She would sit at the kitchen table in the afternoon when her husband was at work in Switzerland and her own children were playing down in the courtyard. She would first call Gretel: 'Come over here, Gretel, sit yourself down!' and after a while she'd send Gretel off and call me: 'Come over here, Monika, sit yourself down, let's have a little think.' I knew exactly what we were supposed to be having a think about. It was of course about our Mutti. But only thinking, not talking about her.

Renate, our little sister, was two years old when our mother died. At the beginning, she slept beside me on my mattress, before she got a little one of her own, a neighbour had one to spare. I have fond memories of us sleeping in the same bed, I love to wallow in nostalgia, when I think about it. She was my doll, and she liked that. She used to say it too with her sweet, hoarse little voice, every evening before going to sleep, she would whisper: 'I'm your doll.' And when she slept at my back, something she especially liked to do, her little tummy against my bottom, she would say: 'You're the steam train and I'm the coal wagon behind.' It was so lovely! When our daughter, Paula, was small, at the age Renate was then, I introduced the idea to her that I was her locomotive and she was my coal wagon, then she used to giggle, and we hugged each other, and she put her little arms around me.

Gretel and I got Renate ready for bed, washed her face, her feet and hands, brushed her teeth, pressed first one nostril shut and then the other so that she had a good nose blow, and lifted her onto the toilet, every evening we did this before going to bed. That was our job, and it was to be our job and remain our job, no one was to interfere. Renate's bladder was our big problem. She could not last the whole night. Gretel used to kneel down at one side of the toilet bowl, with me at the other side. We each held one of Renate's knees and one of her hands firmly and implored her to do a pee-pee. We turned on the tap at the washbasin and made pss-pss-pss noises …

'It's not coming,' said Renate, turning down the corners of her mouth.

Once she had burst into tears about this in front of Uncle Theo, the beer drinker. He said to her: 'You're supposed to let the water come out from down below, not from up top. Have a gulp of beer, then it'll work.'

She had not understood him, it was the first time that he had ever spoken to her. She did not really believe that he was talking to her.

We knew that once we were in the living room and had turned out the light – there was a frosted-glass panel in the door, so secretly putting the light back on was not possible – after that no one was allowed into the bathroom any more. By order of Uncle Theo. Somehow he had succeeded in imposing this ban against Aunt Kathe's wishes. The main snag was that to get to the bathroom, you had to go through the kitchen. There, Uncle Theo would be sitting in his vest, smoking and drinking beer and listening to the news at the top of every hour. The first night, we waited for the news to come on, then we sneaked past behind his back when we thought he wouldn't hear us. But he did hear us and shouted at us angrily. And Renate wept. And Gretel too. I didn't. We were trapped. Aunt Kathe stood fussing over the small hot water tank sitting on top of the stove. I know why I didn't cry. It was because I was thinking: I'm going to tell Uncle Walter and Uncle Sepp and Uncle Lorenz, and they'll give you a good talking to, you in your stupid white singlet! I was focusing on this so intently I imagined Uncle Theo could hear me in his head. The fact that we'd sneaked past had particularly annoyed him. I believe there was a political reason, a compromise: Aunt Kathe had to give way to him on at least one point, otherwise the feeling of being totally under her thumb would have led to one of his outbursts of intense rage, something she feared. And for that reason she stood by the stove pretending to be sorting something out and said nothing.

Renate clamped her little legs together. Often she dribbled on the sheet. We smuggled a porcelain pot into the living room, it was meant to be for milk. No one drank milk in this household, no one noticed the pot was missing. Renate did her business into it. If some went over the rim, we mopped it up with our underwear; it absorbed everything perfectly. Then we chucked the small trickle of pee out of the window. We could hear it splashing onto the pavement. We'd say: what if someone's going past right now, and then giggle ourselves to sleep. Giggling was in general important for us, it meant: we belong together!

I know Gretel often thought about our father too. What was he doing? Where was he? How was he getting on? Was he even still alive? We had now learned that people can die. But because no one talked to us about him, we did not dare to talk to each other about him. Gretel was superstitious and she always found it easy to influence me.

Once she said: 'If you think something, it's there.'

I asked: 'What do you mean?' She must know more than me, I thought, she's older so she must know more.

'If you lay a matchbox on the table, it exists, that's what I mean,' she said. 'So, a thought exists when you think it, you just can't see it, but it's there all the same.'

So I was not under any circumstances to think our father might be dead, dead exactly like our mother. Then the thought would exist and it could come for our father. But how can one manage to *not* think something. Because at precisely that moment one would be thinking about it! I would have liked to have talked to Gretel about it, she seemed to know a thing or two about this topic, but how was I supposed to talk to her about a thought that I was not allowed to think?

I missed our father, and Gretel missed him too. And Renate forgot him. He did not even visit us at Christmas. Nor on New Year's Eve. And Richard we almost forgot as well. How can one almost forget …

Frost patterns formed on the windows. Gretel wanted to sleep with Renate, so we swapped over. I lay on the sofa, a chair placed beside it to stop me falling off in the night, but still I often rolled over the chair onto the floor, when I dreamed about snakes for example. And suffered a few bruises. I counted the flowers on the wallpaper when the moon shone into the living room, counted the twigs on the ash tree in front of the window and the grooves in the wooden arm of the sofa. Until I fell asleep.

Gretel hated the morning gymnastics in front of the open window; I didn't mind it, it was like dancing and Aunt Kathe marked the beat. I surprised myself at how elegantly I could move. If I pretended I was standing on a stage, I forgot the cold. I was a dancer or an actor or both. I threw my head back, as if showing devotion.

Aunt Kathe said: 'Don't exaggerate!'

On New Year's Eve, Uncle Sepp and Uncle Walter arrived. Uncle Walter came with a fat girlfriend and brought two crates of beer – Uncle Sepp a bottle of whisky and chocolates 'for the ladies', that included us too. He handed me an extra praline that he had been given in the chocolate shop for free.

'*Bitte sehr, Mademoiselle*,' he said. 'For you.'

I could smell his aftershave; in the buttonhole of his double-breasted jacket was a white silk rose, at its outside edges you could see tiny threads, like fine hairs. He was wearing his Budapesters again. I had already got him to tell me all about them up on the Tschengla – two-tone shoes with a perforated pattern, black-white, produced in Germany by the firm Heinrich Dinkelacker, I will remember this name as long as I live. 'When winter's over,' he said, 'I'll come and pick you up and we'll go for a stroll along the lakeside.'

I wanted to say: 'I'm only fourteen and I don't have anything to wear.'

'She's going to be a real beauty,' said Uncle Walter's girlfriend, gathering up my hair.

'That's all we need,' said Aunt Kathe. With that, the topic was dropped.

At midnight we were supposed to wish each other a happy New Year. My sisters and my cousins did it properly and got twenty schillings in return. Uncle Walter had had one too many, his money was burning a hole in his pocket, as they say. His banknotes were rolled into a bundle the thickness of an arm and held together by an elastic band from a jam jar. I refused to wish him a happy New Year. I didn't want to have him sticking out his hand to me with the roll of banknotes in it, like he'd done with the other children, looking so pleased with himself, and then with the same self-satisfied look lick the thumb on his other hand and in a quick, throwaway movement, sweep two notes over to me. I hid behind the curtain, like a four-year-old; no fourteen-year-old would do that. That made him furious.

'Come on, say it!' he bellowed.

But it was a different kind of bellowing from the bellowing of Uncle Theo. I could smell the sweat from his armpit. I did not find it unpleasant. It was a family smell and a family bellowing. I thought to myself, a wolf would smell the same. I had never seen a wolf, not even in pictures. I thought a wolf's fur would be like my Uncle Walter's hair, red. On his face one crater clustered next to another – as a young man he had suffered from acne. I liked that. And I wondered what it felt like for his lover when she stroked him.

'Say it!' he bellowed again.

'Leave her alone!' said Uncle Sepp.

Uncle Walter was unsteady on his feet from the beer, he had not wanted to try the whisky, he was supposed to give up all that stuff, he had said to his brother. Again he stretched out the hand with the roll of banknotes in it, pulled out a fifty and flapped the note in front of my nose. I acted unimpressed.

Uncle Sepp said: 'Give her a hundred! If you are going to do it, do it properly!'

'You think I won't do it, don't you? You think I won't do it,' Uncle Walter fired at his tormentor.

'It's your money,' said Uncle Sepp calmly.

Taking out a one hundred schilling note, Walter fanned first his own face, and then mine. As if it were hot, as if it were summer, as if we were lying on the beach at Caorle. I knew that not only did *he* always have one lover after another, but his beautiful plump wife had a lover too, though with her it was always the same one, a representative for an insurance company, with whom she liked to dance the foxtrot in her kitchen. I knew too that the girlfriend Uncle Walter had brought with him today was on the game. I knew this from my older cousin. He had confided in me that he was going to ask Uncle Walter to lend her to him for a quarter of an hour.

'Stop that!' Aunt Kathe stepped in. 'Leave her in peace! She's in a bad mood! She'll soon be back to normal.' And to me: 'A hundred schillings is a lot of money, get that into your head!'

'She'll soon be back to normal,' Uncle Sepp echoed, as he too was afraid the situation might escalate – he knew his brother too well.

'But then it might be too late,' said Walter, and pulled out another hundred. 'My hundred notes are getting homesick.'

I was tempted when I saw the bills right under my nose. How many things could I buy with all that money! But I knew too that both my boy cousins would force me to share and in the end I would get no more than a twenty. If that. The older one had threatened a few days earlier to cut off Gretel's plaits and sell them to a hairdresser he knew. Gretel had clutched both hands to her head, her eyes aghast. Then he took her work basket with her carefully wound, brightly coloured balls of wool, her sewing needles neatly arranged in order, the fine yarns, the crochet hooks and knitting needles, and threw it with all his strength at her head. He would never let me have any of the money, not even a twenty.

And now, listen to this! Walter stretched out the whole wad of money to me. 'And what about this then? What about this? Let's see what happens now! That's a whole month's wages!'

'Stop that now, you idiot,' said Uncle Sepp, and Aunt Kathe said the same thing. Walter gave his brother a shove, he fell against the edge of the table, the Christmas tree toppled over onto the floor, taking me with it, blood ran from my temples down my neck and into my white Sunday blouse. But then – another 'now, listen to this!' – without a moment's hesitation Sepp sprang up and swung at his brother, who was a head taller than him, sending him crashing into the tree, and his month's wages rolled more or less into my lap. I took the roll and threw it, hitting Uncle Walter on the forehead.

In bed, Gretel cursed me for being so stubborn and refusing so much money. 'We could have bought three pairs of tights each.'

'How come *we*?' I said. 'The money would have belonged to me.'

'You could've given a bit to someone else,' she said and turned over noisily to make it clear that she was hurt and angry.

Where do we fit in then? I wondered into my pillow. Can people do what they want with us? Because we don't have a family any more? I'm not a dancing bear! Now even our relatives treat us like fools! Now we belong to no one, absolutely no one. I wanted to wake Gretel up and say to her that of course I would have shared the money with her and Renate, because we belong to each other. But I also wanted to say to her that we are not dancing bears, not for anyone, nor will we be the butt of their jokes. But Gretel was already asleep.

Neither on Christmas Eve nor on New Year's Eve had any mention been made of our father. And what had happened to our brother, Richard? Was he suddenly not one of us any more? Not a word about him. I would have shared the money with him too. I hope, I thought to myself, I do hope Gretel doesn't tell him one day that if I'd kept the money, I would have kept it just for myself.

Renate couldn't get to sleep because she was still so overexcited and asked: 'Who's Mutti?'

'What makes you ask that?' I asked.

'Who is Mutti?' She just repeated the question.

'I'll tell you tomorrow.'

'Why not now?'

'Because I'm too tired and you're tired too.'

'I'm not tired.'

'You are, you just don't realise.'

'I'm not in the least tired. Can I come into your bed?'

She sat up on her mattress and climbed over the chair to get up beside me on the sofa. We didn't have much room. She clung on to me because she was afraid she might fall off.

'Are you my coal wagon?' I asked.

'I'm a big girl now,' she said.

Can you believe it? We had already been in the South Tyrolean Settlement for such a long time and no one had ever said a word to us about our mother or our father! As if we had never had parents, as if we had emerged into the world like buds on a tree. And not once had our father paid us a visit. He had been there one time, unexpectedly, said Aunt Kathe, but we had been in school. He had not wanted to wait. Had left again.

And then Uncle Theo of all people had a talk with me, him of all people. I didn't even count him as one of the family.

It was one of my days of bliss. That meant Wednesday. Aunt Kathe was at the house of a certain Frau Löscher, who had an enormous garden, where she was allowed to harvest as much as she wanted and in return she gave them jam, compote and bottled fruit and vegetables. Our two older cousins were at work, the youngest was somewhere around, Gretel was at swimming lessons and Renate was in kindergarten. The bliss lay in the fact that I was on my own for two to three hours in the apartment and could read or listen to the radio without interruption.

But that day, Uncle Theo was sitting in the kitchen – he had come back from work in the early afternoon. He sat at the table, in front of him a tin of fish, herring in tomato sauce and a beer, a burning cigarette in the ashtray, beside it the packet of cigarettes, one side slit open so that he could always see how many were left.

'I just have to ...' I said.

'Sit down here with me,' he said, his voice was different from usual, gentle – when Gretel and Renate read this, they'll say, impossible. Uncle Theo gentle, impossible. But he really was.

I sat down beside him.

'Do you want a cigarette?' he asked.

'I don't smoke.'

'How am I supposed to know?'

'Well, I'm far too young.'

'I started when I was twelve.'

'Women don't smoke.'

'Huh, don't you believe it!'

'Yes, but less.'

'I've been wanting to say something to you, to you and Gretel,' he sighed – 'hmm, Gretel, hmm, Renate,' he sighed.

'What was it?'

'That I am sorry about everything.'

'About what?'

'About your mama.'

'Thank you.'

'That's what I wanted to say to you.'

'Thank you, Uncle Theo.'

'And something else.'

'What is it?'

'So supposing that …'

'Yes?'

'Supposing … Kathe … supposing Kathe were to die … only supposing, I don't really want to think about it. Then I would …'

'Then what?'

'Do you know how to swim?'

'Gretel has just started learning.'

'That's great. I don't know how to swim. In my day, it was not something we learned. Why would we? Why would we go swimming in the lake? That's crazy. Am I a fish? This is a fish here, now it's lying in tomato sauce, its own fault. It's the same with this ridiculous obsession with eating salad. I'm not a cow for goodness' sake! Kathe always wants me to eat salad, salad, salad, but that's not what I wanted to say. I wanted to say: I would, if Kathe died, I would swim out into the lake on the inflatable mattress, way out, and then I'd pull out the stopper. And that would be that. You know, I can really understand your father. I can't help thinking about what he has gone through and is still going through. It's awful, that … how can I put it … that he is expected to deal with all this. He needs to be looked after. But he refuses. Kathe says he refuses. I sympathise with him. That's what I wanted to tell you.'

'Thank you, Uncle Theo,' I said.

'I just wanted to tell you.'

'Thank you, Uncle Theo.'

'That's OK.'

'Thank you.'

He stubbed out his cigarette in the fish can, plucked a new one from the packet without touching the packet, squeezed it, tapped it and lit it in a rapid movement, the smoke streaming out of his nostrils.

I left the apartment and went for a walk around the area. The windows of some houses were so close to the street that I could look inside, into kitchens where men in vests sat at tables smoking, several with their hats on their heads, everywhere Uncle Theos and the smell of warmed-up leftovers. I thought: I have to get used to it, I have to blend in. This seemed even to me a horribly adult thought, 'conventional' would be the word I would use one year later, then I did not know the word, only a few words made it up to the Tschengla 1,220 metres above sea level. I felt as if I had put on weight and yet was still as thin as a rake.

Uncle Theo lived to a ripe old age; by the end, he looked like a skeleton wrapped in a sheet of yellowing parchment. When my husband and I moved into our house, he stood there swearing and ranting about everything. A friend who was helping us and did not realise that this was the famed Uncle Theo I had so often talked about, said to him, 'Listen, old boy, either you help out, or you shut your trap!' When we were all sitting together later having a beer, Uncle Theo pointed to our friend and said: 'The only one worth his salt around here is him.'

I remember sitting on the steps with my father's prosthetic leg under one arm and cleaning and polishing the shoe at the end of it. The world was small and its treasure trove of words was small, but those words gave a name to everything there was and there was nothing that did not have a name. The forest behind the Home was the forest, the Home was the Home and when the creatures of the night slipped through the tree trunks beneath the moon, we could say it was the creatures of the night that we feared, for in our fear we were not lost for words, for even terror had a name. I felt responsible for the shoe on the prosthesis. That it should look presentable when the disabled guests came. Father and Mother used to take a midday nap, and the prosthesis was then available for me to work on. Often after lunch Mutti would say to him: 'Shall we go up?' That's an expression used in our dialect if one wants to go up into the mountains. My mother meant: shall we go upstairs, into the bedroom on the next floor, and have a lie down? Then they would smile at each other, our parents, and didn't bother too much about us any more. What could possibly happen to us 1,220 metres above sea level! Father unbuckled the prosthesis and Mother placed it outside the door. Like in a smart hotel. I was the shoeshine girl.

The very next day, after the meeting with Uncle Theo in his 'nicotine-spaceship' – that was a term invented by Uncle Lorenz, a reference to the Russian sputnik – Aunt Kathe took the decision that we were to visit our father. In our Sunday best. Of course both Gretel and I had been longing to see Vati, but now I didn't want to go. The Sunday clothes were to blame. Why Sunday clothes? Maybe he'd give me a whack on the head. He wouldn't put up with me contradicting him. Sunday clothes could only mean he had become estranged from us. The next thing would be that we'd have to address him formally as *Sie*. He was sure to ask me if I liked living with Aunt Kathe and I would say no, and he'd ask whether we missed him, and again I would say no, and he'd ask if I missed Mutti, and again I would shake my head, and then I'd get a walloping. I knew that I had such a terrible compulsion in me to be contrary.

And then Gretel asked: 'Where is he actually?'

I had wanted to see our father so badly and not once had I asked myself where he was! As if he were somewhere omnipresent in the air, and if we were to call him, he would appear. A spirit. One of the creatures of the night we had been scared of, but not all that scared, for we had never seen them nor had we ever called out to them.

And so I asked as well: 'Where is he actually?'

'Don't always repeat everything your sister says like a parrot!' said Aunt Kathe. That was mean. The 'always' was mean. I never parroted what Gretel said.

We got no answer.

I resisted. Stuck my arms out straight as if to stop it all. Just to be difficult, I did not take an umbrella and refused to go under my big sister's umbrella. Renate, who had no idea what was going on, wore her raincoat and sniffed her snotty nose constantly, a welcome sound for me that afternoon – an anthem for our three-girl republic. Aunt Kathe had written the address down for us and drew a map of how to get there on a sheet of paper that she tore out of my school notebook. But she told us nothing about what awaited us at our destination. Just that we should ring the bell.

It was a convent.

Please, for heaven's sake, no, surely our father has not gone into a monastery! Uncle Walter made jokes about it later: 'Our old mate, Josef, crept under the skirt tails of the nuns!' He nearly got a whack from Aunt Kathe. Our father was going through a bad patch. That is the phrase Aunt Kathe used.

The Sisters of Mercy had made a room available for him. A cell. We were not allowed to enter. He did not want us to. But I had a glance inside – a camp bed, a small table, too small to spread a newspaper out on, a hard chair, a chest of drawers on which stood a grey tin washbasin. That was it. No curtains at the window. Toilet and water tap down the corridor. His encyclopaedia, ten volumes, *Brehm's Life of Animals* and the *Kosmos* magazines he subscribed to, were lined up by his bed. Above the bed hung the Saviour on a bare wall, not even nailed to the cross. On the chest of drawers, a glass half full of water and a little tube of pills. One of the sisters had knocked and, without waiting for a reply, opened the door.

'Josef, your children.'

There he sat. Shoulders sloping downwards as if wedges had been sawn off to the right- and left-hand sides of his neck. A knitted cardigan. Bluish. Gretel and I stood at the open door, Renate between us. I felt cold and thought to myself, I know why this man looks so thin: it's because on the Tschengla as manager of the Convalescent Home for War-wounded, he always used to wear a jacket, and the jacket had padded shoulders, and here in the convent he has no choice but to show his true self, here there's no way of hiding it. He sat on the bed, his legs did not quite reach the ground, above his knee I could see the lump where the prosthesis was attached. Was the bed so high or was he so small? I felt cold and I thought: he's shrunk. He looked at me as if to apologise, as if he wanted to make up for it and grow again as soon as possible.

'Where's Richard?' he asked. That was the first thing he said.

'At Aunt Irma's,' said Gretel.

'Is he doing well?'

'Better than we are, I'm sure,' I burst out.

'Why's that? What's wrong?'

'Monika means Uncle Theo smokes too much,' said Gretel.

'That's not what I mean at all,' I objected.

'What do you mean then?'

'Just saying,' I said, and was scared and not scared that he would immediately start criticising my grammar, that I should think before I speak and so on, that 'Just saying' was not a proper sentence but a nonsensical remark expressing nothing but one's stupidity. When irritated by a linguistic blunder, he could be very hurtful.

But he said: 'I'm sorry. I really am truly sorry.'

'It's OK,' I said. I got this from my older cousin, he used to say 'OK' instead of 'yes'. That appealed to me.

'And how about you?' he asked Renate.

She glanced first at Gretel, then at me. I nodded at her, and she said: 'Not too bad,' and glanced back again to Gretel and to me.

'My girls,' he said.

'Next time should we bring you something?' asked Gretel.

He didn't answer. 'Go into the kitchen, there's something there for you.'

'A dessert again?' I asked.

We had already trooped partway down the corridor, hesitant and bewildered, when he called after us, standing half out of the door: 'The things you're wearing, who do they belong to? I tell you: they're not yours. Even the dirt under your fingernails is not yours – you scratched it out from someone else's window frame. Listen closely! No, not *come* closer, I said: *Listen* closely! I said nothing about "coming closer". But you still have a little bit of something that belongs to you. That's good. That's good. But watch out! When you have almost nothing, you can quickly get to the point where you think it's better to have absolutely nothing at all. Then you lose what little you have, or you give it away, or you throw it out. Wrong! Absolutely wrong! Why? I'll tell you why! Listen closely! Stay where you are but listen closely! When you have absolutely nothing left, absolutely nothing is of any value to you any more. Even your own self seems worthless to you. And then all the floodgates are open. Don't forget that!'

And he was already back in his cell.

That was the longest speech I had ever heard from my father. Gretel and I were now even more dispirited and bewildered. Truth be told, I did not dare ask

Gretel if she'd heard what I'd heard. I felt shaken. I thought, I don't know our father at all. Really, not at all. His face was so white, it made me feel ill. I would never eat anything here, I thought, even if they forced it on me.

We were offered stewed apples, strained through a sieve into a fine purée, lukewarm. Gretel fed Renate, who slurped happily, a biscuit in each hand. The Sister Superior observed us from a distance. Renate's snot mingled with the apple purée. We were not taken back to Vati's cell, we had forgotten to say goodbye.

On the way home, we dragged our feet. Gretel said we were not allowed to go by the path through the forest, because a child had been murdered there a few weeks previously. This I found intriguing and wanted her to tell me about it. She said, not in front of Renate. It had been indescribably grue-some, indescribably. The little girl toddled between us, we could have gone anywhere with her, onto a ship and off overseas – overseas, what a marvellous word! We didn't talk about our father. I suspected Gretel was thinking the same thing as me. Why had he not replied when we asked if we should bring him something next time? Does he not want us to visit him again? It occurred to me, I didn't know why, it just occurred to me out of the blue, how our Mutti and Aunt Irma had sometimes sat together on the terrace and without any discussion had begun singing together, and then a song came into my head

that had been my favourite, a lullaby in local dialect,
I hummed, Gretel joined in:

> Sleep my little mousie,
> Day is slipping off its shoes
> And towards those high Swiss mountains
> It flits on tippy toes.
>
> Don't you fear my darling
> The valley's now in shadow.
> God's lighting up a thousand lamps
> High up in Heaven's meadow.
>
> And in the lantern of the moon
> He puts a candle bright
> To help Him better watch my boy
> And keep him safe all night.

That had been so beautiful.

In Quellenstrasse, we came across a prostitute –
back then, I thought she was old, but she was at
most forty – we recognised her and greeted her,
and she returned our greeting. We knew exactly
how she earned her living, Uncle Walter had filled us
in, with so much detail that Aunt Kathe had finally
rapped a spoon on the kitchen table and all the grinning mouths round it were hastily readjusted. The
way the woman was sitting there made me think that
she had nothing either, even less than we did; we at
least have a little bit of something, the little glass ring

that I got as a gift from my mother and is too small for my finger now, for example. This woman here, the only thing that can no longer be taken from her is what she has just swallowed, this woman has nothing, like the nothingness father spoke about, half out of his cell. All that belongs to her is her bare skin. She was sitting on a folding chair, waiting for customers. It was no longer raining, over towards Switzerland in the west was a last glimpse of blue sky, the sun was already over the mountains. Renate dragged her raincoat along behind her, we didn't tell her not to.

'Off home, then?' called the woman.

'Yes,' said Gretel.

'Home is the nicest place, isn't it?'

'Yes,' said Gretel.

'Hey, come over here, my darlings!' the woman called after us. 'Let's have a look at you.'

We turned around and stood in front of her, Renate in the middle. The woman remained sitting, she had enormous breasts and had opened her blouse wide so that their full contours could be seen from afar.

'I've forgotten your names,' she said.

'But we never told you them,' I said.

'You should always take a second name,' she said. 'No need for everyone to know who you are. Do you want a lipstick? I've got a whole heap of them to spare. Someone left them here for me.'

We said we would really like one. But she didn't give us one. It was too much trouble for her to get up, she said, it wasn't worth the effort. If we came tomorrow, she would definitely have one ready for all three of us. I was thinking, the lipsticks don't even belong to you, it's easy to give things away if you don't have anything. We carried on walking. I already knew almost everything about sex, our older cousin used to take me aside and talk about it openly. He described to me exactly what sex was, so I knew what this woman did and also that she got money for it, to buy food for herself. And I thought, that's handy, she doesn't need anything except her own self. And if I were nice to men, they would be nice to me too. What goes around comes around. The only thing I'd need would be soap and you can get that for free; in the drugstore you can get free samples. The woman was not good looking, but she wasn't ugly either, she had a bit of a belly, but it looked attractive; I would never have one like that. If I were her, I would get myself a stock of soap. I could not think of any other job where the main focus was on being nice to each other.

Just at that moment, I swear, precisely at that moment, as if she had been thinking exactly the same as me, Gretel said: 'Monika, can I ask you something?' Much later I asked her if she still remembered this encounter, she said, of course she remembered and that she had thought then, it couldn't be that bad going on the game. Exactly like me.

'Ask me what?' I'd replied.

'What do you think Vati meant,' she answered, 'when he said: "Then all the floodgates are open"? I'm wondering, because he said we shouldn't forget.'

'Oh, nothing in particular,' I said, waving my hands around, 'I have a vague idea but I don't know exactly either, doesn't really matter, he's just gone a bit loopy, he'll be fine.'

With that she was happy. Or maybe not. It was clear to both of us that our father could not go on like this. For him, the floodgates were open. He was being swept downstream. I am not quite sure whether I had any idea at that time what floodgates were. But I knew that our father was drifting further and further away, and if something was not done, and done quickly, he would not come through this. He needed a new wife. We didn't need a new Mutti, that wouldn't be possible anyway. I had heard Aunt Kathe saying exactly the same thing to her brothers, Walter, Sepp and Lorenz. 'Josef needs a wife!' Word for word. Gretel and Renate heard it too. A new wife does not automatically mean a new mother. The prostitute with the big bosom would surely be a good new wife for our father, I thought. It was her profession, being loving. That's what was sorely needed. And she wouldn't need to learn the ropes first, like another woman might. She had it all sorted. And we wouldn't automatically have to call her Mutti, or Mama either. She definitely wouldn't want that. The way she spoke made us feel, at least Gretel and me, that she was speaking to us woman to woman, perhaps not exactly that yet, but once she was our father's new wife, there could be three women in the new family: her, Gretel and me, and soon even four women, when Renate was old enough. She could give us good tips when we were going out for the evening and wanted to make ourselves look good. She could give us good tips about talking to a boy, how we should play up to him, flirt with him, drive him crazy, but also how to give him the brush-off if we didn't find him attractive, if he was too dim or didn't clean his teeth properly or talked a load of nonsense. This would be the best solution for our Vati, and for us too, I thought, and got quite excited about the idea. Only I didn't know how to explain it to Aunt Kathe. She would threaten to give me a whack. Maybe it would be best, I thought, if I spoke to Uncle Walter about it first. He'd see that it made sense. He would be all for it. He'd say, that's the best solution. I would just have to impress upon him that he shouldn't tell on me. The idea that Vati should marry the nice prostitute should not come from me, it should come from him. That was the first thing. Secondly: someone had to talk to the prostitute. What if she said no? I didn't really think she would. Not because she was longing to take on a family of four at one hit – Richard would of course come too – but because she had looked at us in such a warm and friendly way. She would think to herself, well, it's not ideal, so many kids all at once, but they looked at me in a warm and friendly way, perhaps that's enough. I was sorry that I had been snippy when she had – in a roundabout way – asked our names. I resolved to go and see her the following day, first to apologise to her, and then to ask if she had half an hour to spare for me, and then to truly open up my heart to her, tell her honestly every last detail.

I seem to remember that I spoke to Gretel about it on the way home, a few first allusions. Today she laughs out loud at this.

'Never! Come on, what do you think my response would have been!'

I call Renate in Berlin and ask her, she was with us too – yes, she was still quite small, but she was there, she must have heard what we were saying. And she would have understood what Gretel and I were speaking about, she always pricked up her ears when we were talking about something that sounded grown-up.

She says: 'Yes, I think so, yes, I think I do remember.'

'What do you remember?' I ask.

'Well, just that you spoke to Gretel about it.'

'About what?'

'Whether Vati could be paired off with that woman.'

'You're just making that up now,' I say. 'You'd like that idea. Now he's no longer alive. Now you feel you can say things like that.'

'I'm sure he would have let himself be paired off,' said Renate. 'And she was so nice. I remember that so clearly, that she looked at us in such a warm and caring way. And I remember that it was you who was a bit nasty to her. She would have been caring to Vati. Yes, I think she would have married him.'

Now I am the one to get furious. 'Never!' I shout down the receiver.

'And this is where the story first begins,' said my stepmother. 'At any rate, my story.'

We were still sitting at her kitchen table, although two hours ago we had agreed to go for a walk, that is, she had asked me whether I would go with her, she had promised the doctor to walk for one hour every day, come rain or shine. Joints, blood pressure, cholesterol, lungs. In the meantime, she had put a slab of butter, a chunk of cheese, a stick of sausage and some bread on the table. 'You know where to find the cutlery and the chopping board.'

'Do you want a beer?' she asked.

'Do you have a gulp of red wine?' And in that moment, I recalled what my father would have said to that: you want a gulp of red wine? Aha. Do you know what a gulp is? One can only describe something as a gulp when liquid has passed over the palate. Now picture please what happens if I serve you a gulp of red wine! – Yes, honestly, his nitpicking got on my nerves, it made me want to scream! Even today I still hear him in my head. Many a time I have heard him in my mind challenging me about a text, as I sat at the typewriter or later at the computer, and he still does it today, whenever I am trying to describe a scene in a story. I write a sentence and I can hear him saying: Aha? How would you define that then? This was the reason I never gave him any of my writings in progress to read. He lived to see my first two books, a collection of stories and a novel, and I brought him a copy of each with a dedication – 'For Vati, who is to blame for my love of books' and 'For Vati, look, my name is on the spine'. I was moved, the whole evening he sat there with the books in his hands, stroked them, sniffed at them, opened them at random and with eyebrows raised read a paragraph, without comment. The next time I came to visit, I saw that he had placed my books on the shelf for German-language authors, quite an honour being placed immediately after Heinrich Heine!

My stepmother poured us both a glass of red wine, I declined her offer of a cigarette, saying for at least the tenth time, honestly for the tenth time: 'Not for the last twenty-five years, thank you,' and leaning over the table to light hers with the lighter.

'I tried taking snuff instead for a while,' she said. 'But it's not the same. Would be healthier for the lungs, but it's not the same.'

'Have you ever not smoked?' I asked.

'Of course,' she laughed, 'from ages one to twenty.'

'I mean, have you never given up in between?' I could see it then. She had been infected by our father's obsession with dissecting language, that answer could have come from him.

'Yes, I have, but that's not what I wanted to talk to you about.'

She wanted to tell me about herself, about the role she played in our father's story. But she had to backtrack a bit, and first report what had become of Aunt Irma.

So, Aunt Irma had married this remarkable man, Pirmin. The blind colossus. The masseur, whom the hopeless cases went to. Those he led into the basement, where he turned the radio up loud, so that their screams would be drowned out. He used to hand the client the schnapps bottle to relieve the pain – I know this from my husband, who was treated by him when he had hardly been able to sit down because of excruciating back pain. Pirmin had approached Irma's brother Lorenz, and asked for her hand. As he thought was the proper thing to do. Lorenz was not the oldest of the siblings, that was Heinrich, Aunt Kathe too was older, but for Pirmin, Lorenz was the head of the family. He was undoubtedly the brightest, particularly when it came to numbers, but above all he had a presence. When first his father and then his mother died, he had been only just sixteen. He and Kathe had made sure that the Bagage did not go under. Pirmin had asked for a meeting to be set up with Lorenz. Irma wrote a letter to her brother, telling him that she had a boyfriend, and could her boyfriend ask him something. There was no harm in asking, answered Lorenz and confirmed a date.

When Pirmin took hold of my Aunt Irma, his hands covered her chest and her back. With bowed head – my stepmother told me that Aunt Irma had told her – he had stood before Lorenz and had said: 'Lorenz, I want to marry your sister. Give me your blessing!'

Lorenz said: 'I don't have a blessing, but there's one thing you need to know: if you ever hit her, Sepp will kill you.'

That was a joke. An allusion that Pirmin had no way of comprehending. Irma would get it. For when our Vati married our Mutti, Uncle Sepp had said this same sentence, but in fun; he had wanted to show that his sister Grete was his favourite, and Vati had taken it in exactly that spirit.

'That's fantastic!' rejoiced Pirmin. 'I'm so pleased. I expected nothing less! That's how things should be! That's family! Let me be one of your family!' and more in that vein.

Afterwards Lorenz said to his sister Kathe, and his brothers, Heinrich, Walter and Sepp: 'He talks a lot and loudly. Apart from that there's nothing much to object to about him. I said yes.'

But soon there was in fact something to object to. Just one year after the wedding.

Irma, her thick plait of hair coiled round her head, was gripping her dress tightly, her fists clutching the flowery material: she had found out that her husband was involved with a woman from Styria, that he was, as he liked to call it, 'painting' this hussy. She had imagined — so my stepmother told me that Irma had told her — she had imagined herself stubbing out twenty cigarettes right in the middle of the bastard's forehead and his whore's, a circle for each of them just where the priest rubs ash in the sign of the cross on Ash Wednesday. She had gargled with Odol mouthwash and scrubbed her fingers at least ten times a day. She felt so disgusted. It was 1963, it was announced on the news that Kennedy, the American president, had been shot. 'Well,' Irma had later confessed to my stepmother, 'for two pins, I'd have got my gun out too.'

No longer knowing which way to turn, she reached out to her brothers and sisters, and they came to help her. The brothers confronted the blind colossus and he began to sob, unbelievably loudly, so loudly that a neighbour rang the police. He dropped to his knees in front of the two officers and shouted that he admitted everything: he was a bastard, they should take him now and lock him up, they would just be doing him a favour, no one in the world had the right to be such a bastard as he was, not even someone who'd suffered in life as he had, first an avalanche had swept away the family home with all of them inside, father, mother, brother, sister all dead, and then on top of that he became blind, and then, what was he to do about it, God, in His mysterious way, had then struck him with this damned sex drive, that made him behave like a bastard ... and so on.

The scene must have been quite impressive. The policemen made the sign of the cross. Not because they thought it was the devil kneeling before them. But the Man of Sorrows in person. Made flesh in a man six foot six inches tall with white eyeballs, and hands that one would not wish anyone to feel round their neck. Irma's brothers Lorenz, Walter and Sepp – Heinrich had stayed home, he didn't want to interfere – had come to give their brother-in-law a fright, each of them with a knife in his trouser pocket, now they all stood quite still. And when Pirmin turned his backside to them and pleaded with them to at least give him a kick up the arse with their hobnailed boots, they didn't oblige. Uncle Sepp said: 'We don't have hobnailed boots. We're not farmers any more. I've got my Italian loafers on, calfskin from Milan.'

The brothers together with Aunt Kathe took Irma aside. They put pressure on her. She should get divorced. He himself said he was a bastard, a sex maniac, who couldn't stop himself. She would suffer all her life with this man, he was never the right man for her, she was just five foot three in height and delicate. Aunt Irma said she would think about it.

'I know,' said my stepmother, 'you got to know a different Irma up on the Tschengla. A woman who would never have put up with such behaviour.'

'That's true,' I said.

'That was just how she saw herself inside her head. I don't want to repeat to you everything that went on inside her head. She told me all about it and I said, stop, Irma, I don't want to listen to all that. And I told her, she should never speak to anyone about it; you can rely on me, I said, I won't tell anyone else. Just keep your mouth shut, or they'll lock you away in the madhouse. But she was only like that inside her head. She allowed Pirmin to get away with everything. In the real world, the world outside her head.'

Our father liked Pirmin. He amused him. Even his vulgar talk didn't bother him, if anything the opposite was true. Pirmin was what in my youth I would have called a freak. And this appealed to our father. My elder son, Oliver, would say: a totally crazy guy. Pirmin, like our father, had been expected to become a priest. Because he, like my father, was intelligent. An intelligent bastard, a preacher. Whenever he'd had a bit too much to drink, he stomped around, marching into the furniture, which flew right and left like startled hares as he quoted from the Latin liturgy. *Gloria in excelsis Deo. Et in terra pax hominibus bonae voluntatis.* A voice like rolling thunder. At church, when he sang 'Holy God, we praise Thy name', the crown of thorns on the head of the Lord Jesus beside the altar trembled. I have already said that I seldom saw my father laugh but whenever Uncle Pirmin came to visit us, he always laughed.

Incidentally, the woman from Styria mentioned previously remained his lover all his life. After twenty years, he had a second house built in the garden for her. He lived together with two women – but this by no means meant that he remained faithful to them. After his death, his lover became bedbound and Aunt Irma cared for her until the end. Before Aunt Irma's death, I visited her one last time. She was frail and thin, light enough to be blown away, hardly present any more. She died in her late seventies, her eyesight was poor, her legs were bad, but her mental state was as sharp as ever, and her choice of words hurtful. The Bagage family, those who were still alive, went to her funeral. She lies in a small cemetery, very pretty, in the middle of Ried, in a little Romanesque church surrounded by a wall, an open ossuary right by the entrance, piled up with old skulls that grin at you. As I stood with the few mourners by her grave – Aunt Kathe was there, Uncle Sepp, my sister Gretel – the image came to me of her being reborn as a piece of gravel, because she was so sharp. As a girl, she had black hair, long, shining, the mark of the Bagage. In later life, she wore her hair plaited and pinned in a braid around her head. In spite of her limited wardrobe, she still managed to make something of herself. But there was always a dagger in her eyes. It was easy to be fooled by her delicateness. Our mother did not consider it necessary for us to have baths in cold water, she said that just thinking about it made her feel frozen. She filled a tub in the kitchen for us, turned on the oven, it was as warm as if it were high summer. Gretel and I stood in the bathtub, one after the other, and were soaped down and dried off. When Aunt Irma came by, she said, a child had to be toughened up to survive in life.

'The plan,' continued my stepmother, 'was as follows. Lorenz had worked it out and they were all in agreement. Irma should get divorced from Pirmin, then remain single for a year, as is right and proper, and then marry your father. So that he gets back on his feet.'

'And did they ask Vati? Whether he even wanted to?'

'I have no idea. But I guess he would have accepted her. He accepted me after all.'

This was a tricky topic. I thought it best not to say anything. It is not necessary to know every last detail, and if you don't know every last detail, then when telling the story, you can always make everything sound better than it was, which is much harder if you do know everything.

'In a way, that would have made sense,' continued my stepmother. 'There are countries where that's the custom. You probably know that better than me. If the husband dies, his brother marries his wife, and vice versa if the wife dies, her sister marries her husband. And then of course there was Richard too. Irma looked after him after your mother's death. I don't know if he even remembered your Mutti at all. If he did, it was only vaguely. Irma was Mama to him.

Not a bad mama. Pirmin was jealous of the lad, she was so fond of him. He had a better time of it than you did in the South Tyrolean Settlement. Irma baked something for him twice a week, *Bienenstich* cake, poppyseed cake or nut strudel. He had his own room. His own little transistor radio. She practised reading and writing with him before he even started school. She read aloud to him. And played board games with him. On Sundays he was allowed to stay up late and listen to the detective drama on the radio. At first, she tried to keep him out of Pirmin's way, told Richard he should keep very quiet, Uncle Pirmin was blind, he wouldn't see him, but then Pirmin sniffed the air and bellowed: I smell human flesh. Irma was a really good mama for Richard. It was more or less considered a given that she would take on your father. But she didn't want to.'

'Did she say outright that she didn't want to marry Vati? That she didn't want him?'

'She said that she didn't want to get divorced from Pirmin. That's not quite the same thing. Nevertheless, end of discussion.'

We paused for some time. Because it was obvious what had to come next.

'So then?' I asked finally.

'Ah, yes. Then ...' said my stepmother.

Uncle Sepp had been the one to insist they could no longer carry on watching Josef go to the dogs. And also he had whispered a promise into Grete's ear on her deathbed, that he would watch out for him. And since Irma did not want to marry our father, they had to look elsewhere. Was there another woman who might be suitable? And they found someone. A cousin. Her mother and my maternal grandmother were sisters. They had grown up in better circumstances. Not that their circumstances were great, just that they were better. Mind you, that didn't take much. Ottilie had a career in front of her. As a dressmaker. Following her apprenticeship, she had become a master tailor, and after that had moved to Switzerland, to Geneva. She learned French and had found a position in a large tailoring business, where big-name designers had their garments made. She was one of the best in the team. She intended at some point soon to start her own workshop. Marriage and childbearing were not in her thoughts. Maybe one day. But for now work came first. She was passionate about her work, and she loved her freedom, for example walking along the lakeside in the morning before work, sitting down in the Café du Centre, the first one to open, ordering a *café noir* and a croissant and reading a French newspaper – it didn't matter which one, as long as it was French. Freedom also meant sitting in front of the open window in the evening, with her feet up on the window ledge, drinking a Pernod and smoking a cigarette in a cigarette holder. And why not? If you're on your own, you can do as you please.

Her goal was Paris. She felt confident that she would have the nerve to knock on Coco Chanel's door and ask her if she could come and work for her. She still believed that this was the only way to go about it. She collected offcuts of material, stuck them in an album and labelled them. And she collected buttons too. She had a huge chest full of buttons, a treasure trove. I secretly hoped to inherit the chest after her death, but it wasn't there any more.

And Uncle Sepp had also been the one who had persuaded her.

'It's funny it was him, the one person who hardly ever opened his mouth!' I remarked incredulously.

He had volunteered.

'That sounds like when there is a disaster response,' I said.

'That's exactly what it was.'

He had driven to Geneva on his motorbike and had waited at her door.

I wanted to know. I had always wanted to know how our father had come by a new wife. 'How did he win you over?'

'Oh, you don't need every last detail,' she said. 'Why don't you have a cigarette with me, then I wouldn't feel so guilty.'

'You'd feel even more guilty if I started again!'

Our Vati remarried and got back on his feet. Uncle Lorenz, who had previously arranged the room with the Sisters of Mercy, now arranged a job for him in the tax office. And because he had his Matura school-leaving certificate and was an intelligent man anyway, he rose up through the ranks and finally, that is after a few years, he was made manager of the personnel department. He fetched his four children back home, Gretel, Renate and me, and Richard, and he fathered one more son and a daughter. We were back in a cramped space. Back in an apartment in Vorkloster, not far from the South Tyrolean Settlement, four rooms.

Each time the word 'stepmother' comes up when I am writing, I stop short, and think I should leave out the 'step'. Because it is unfair. Stepmothers in fairy tales, stepmothers in jokes. And because I have a guilty conscience towards her even today. She wanted us to call her by her first name. Our father wanted us to call her Mutti. Gretel kicked up a fuss. I kicked up a fuss too. And then Renate kicked up a fuss as well. Richard said he didn't know what was going on any more, he wanted to go back to Aunt Irma. She did not want to be a substitute and could not be a substitute, she said. In just fifteen minutes, poison filled the air. But there was no agreement. She said this was all preposterous. I didn't know the meaning of this word and looked it up in the dictionary that night and wrote it into my secret vocabulary notebook. Gretel and I, and Richard too, avoided calling her anything. Renate was the first to call her Mutti. After that we did too. And then I had a guilty conscience again, and still have it today, because of our real Mutti. Our father never referred to his second wife by that name. He could for example have said: go and help your Mutti in the kitchen! He never did.

Uncle Lorenz and Uncle Sepp visited us often, seldom together. Aunt Kathe lived the closest, but we hardly saw her, only on birthdays and at Christmas and New Year. When Uncle Lorenz came, there were discussions about politics – that the 'Blacks', the Austrian People's Party, only looked after their own but that the Gorbach government was about to go under – and about history too. Uncle Lorenz did not read novels, he only read non-fiction, mainly historical works, on the French Revolution, about Bismarck, about Lenin, about the Nazi period. My father listened, made brief comments from time to time, seldom contradicted. They also exchanged books – with Uncle Lorenz, my father could have confidence that he would be careful with them. I was sometimes allowed to sit with them, but at a distance, I was not allowed to speak. I was amazed by the way that Uncle Lorenz imparted his knowledge. It sounded as if he was exchanging views with someone else, even though he was actually holding a monologue. So he might say: 'Ah, now I understand you! I see what you mean!' but no one had said anything. Or: 'To that I would just make the following point!' But again, no one had said anything. There were evenings when he was the only one to speak, absolutely the only one, as if the rest of us had made an agreement not to open our mouths, and yet when he was leaving, he would say: 'Thank you, Josef, it's so stimulating for me having a conversation with you.'

When Uncle Sepp visited us, the evenings were very quiet. He and my father played chess. I don't know which of them was better, eventually the game would end and it was never mentioned who had won or who had lost. And when Uncle Sepp was leaving, he didn't say anything, maybe muttered something. Perhaps the mutter meant: 'Thank you, Josef, it's so stimulating being silent with you.' How had this handsome man with his modest manners and his impeccable wardrobe succeeded in persuading a woman with a budding career to marry a disabled man who had four children – I can speculate about this all night, I cannot fathom it! Sepp himself had so little luck in love! His brother Walter, the woman-whisperer, passed on to him a prostitute he had hung around with for a while – not as her pimp but as a lover in the normal sense – and my shy Uncle Sepp married this woman. Why did he do that? Uncle Lorenz ranted at him (this was at our house), Uncle Walter ranted at him, Aunt Kathe pleaded with him – to no avail. The woman made him unhappy. She carried on plying her trade, he did not want her money, he gave her all his salary and kept back only some pocket money. He brought his beautiful suits to our stepmother for mending and pressing. But then he got a divorce. Uncle Lorenz came with a five-litre bottle of Sekt sparkling wine, Uncle Walter with a hog, we barbecued it down by the lake and toasted Uncle Sepp, but a year later he married the same woman again.

And Uncle Walter? He was the man who gave generous tips. Even if he had only a small cup of coffee and cream in a coffee bar, he would leave a tip of double the amount. One anecdote relates how he once took the train to Zurich, to throw himself into the nightlife there, but on his way back found the trains had stopped running. It was close to Christmas and cold and he had not wanted to hang around, so he hailed a taxi. The driver said: you know of course what that's going to cost you, all the way to Austria. My Uncle Walter then flagged down a second taxi, laid his hat on the back seat and directed them to take him home in convoy, him in the front, the hat behind.

Many years ago, I was with my husband in New York. While strolling through Harlem on 134th Street, I came across a flight of steps, wedged between a barber's and a launderette, leading down into a shop. Above the door, it said: 'MYSTERY MEN'. It was dark down there and it took a minute for my eyes to adjust. It smelled dusty. There were shelving units stacked against the walls but there were some standing in the middle of the room as well, on which lay figures and parts of figures, arms, legs, heads, made from wood, clay, iron and plastic. Right at the back, a little light penetrated through a narrow window. I saw someone bending over, his back to me.

I said: 'Hello?' I called to the man a few times before he turned around. He was very old and black, his skull bald and shiny.

I asked whether I might have a look around.

He said: 'No, no! Forbidden!' Then he indicated to me to step closer.

My husband had followed me but had remained standing at the door. He made a sign to me. Let's go. I shook my head.

The old man took my hand and moved it across the surface of the table, to and fro, to and fro. As if he were blind. Finally he took an object from the shelf, simply reached for it without looking, and laid it in my open hand: a figure. About the size of the span between my little finger and thumb.

'Little dad, very old,' said the man.

The figure was made of wood. It was black, felt silky to the touch, really smooth. Its head was round except for the face, which was flat, with closed eyes, a nose, a mouth, and carved ears, and it had a solid neck, slanting shoulders like a cape, chest, arms, hands with fine fingers, a narrow body, a small penis, short stubby legs and feet with no toes. The man took the figure from my hand again, placed it on the table, turned it. I could see the other side, smooth with protruding buttocks, the calves, the ankles.

I asked the price. It was so high that I thought I must have misheard. I thanked him and walked towards the exit.

I heard him call: 'Lady,' he said, 'come on, I will redeem you!'

My husband was waiting at the door and signalled to me again. At the time we were both very raw emotionally because our daughter had died – struck dead by a rock while on a hike. The old man handed the figure to me. The price which he now quoted, I was able to afford. Before I could get my money out of my bag, my husband gave him a banknote, more than the price demanded, and pulled me out of the shop.

In the light of day, the figure gleamed – sometimes my husband held it in his hands – sometimes I held it in mine. We returned southwards to our hotel on East 42nd Street, just a few steps away from the UN building. We laughed about his tiny penis. On our way back, we continued to take turns holding the figure – sometimes it nestled in his hand, then in mine. At night I laid it on my pillow. I clasped the smooth head and fell asleep.

I told my husband, when I die, you have to put the figure in my coffin. Once, as I was shaking out my bedcover back at home, the figure that I call 'little Papa' fell out of the window. One foot broke off.

I was inconsolable because I couldn't find the foot. The figure had fallen onto rough gravel.

One day, by chance, my husband found the foot. He glued it back on, and since then I take good care of little Papa and he takes good care of us. I hope so anyway. We speak to our children on the phone, to Oliver, Undine, Lorenz, and we talk about Paula often.

'You're ashamed to be with me, aren't you!' said my father. When was that? Was I fifteen? Or already sixteen? No older. We were living together with him and my stepmother – some good times, some bad times, some bad times, some good times. He pushed his bicycle to the edge of the road. 'You go in front,' he said.

I came up behind him with my bike; it was summer, I wore a dress with a rose pattern and sandals with bare feet.

'Come on, go past me, get going!' he snapped. He stood there in his eternal trousers, his right leg stiff. He was still able to ride a bicycle well, using just one foot; it was held by a strap onto the left pedal so that he could push and pull, the right pedal didn't turn.

'No, you go ahead!' I said. 'Let's have a race! See who gets to the sanatorium first!'

A race on the road through the woods, where the trees nodded a greeting. 'Don't even think about letting me win,' he added crossly, 'that would be the end of our friendship.' And he said that in all serious-ness. Was my father ever my friend? I almost asked him that.

I overtook him, which any child could have done, my skirt flapped past his handlebars. I could hear him panting behind me and slowed down a bit. He caught up.

'Shall I tell you about a dream that the writer Gustave Flaubert wrote down?' he wheezed.

'Do you have to?' I said. I enjoyed listening to him, he was very knowledgeable, but I also enjoyed contradicting him.

'Yes, young lady, I have to!' he said.

'In the middle of a cycle race, you want to tell me what a writer dreamed about?'

'Yes, I do. In the middle of a cycle race.'

We were going more slowly and so close beside each other that he had trouble keeping his balance.

'Keep your distance!' he commanded. 'Are you listening?'

'I'm trying.'

'Perhaps it's better to leave it.'

'All right, leave it.'

'Would be interesting though.'

'Get on with it then!'

'So, Flaubert went into the forest with his mother and some monkeys came and encircled them. There were more and more of them. One of them stroked Flaubert who got really scared. He took his gun and shot it in the shoulder. The monkey was bleeding and fell to the ground. Then his mother said to him: why on earth did you do that? It was being gentle with you, it wanted to be your friend.'

'Why are you telling me this now?' I asked.

'It just seems quite apt, for us and the forest.'

We rode on further. We rode side by side, not speaking. Workmen were mending the road and whistled at me. I really liked that, it lifted my spirits.

'You should wear trousers when you're cycling,' said my father, 'that would be more suitable.'

'Suitable for what?'

'For not attracting attention.'

'I like attracting attention. Anyway some trousers attract attention too.'

'Are you ashamed of me?' he asked again.

'Tell me,' I said, as we sat on the bench in front of the sanatorium, 'what else did your Flaubert dream about?'

'Well, he was sure that crazy people and animals had a special liking for him.'

'Because of the monkey dream?'

'Probably he just wanted to show off. Like you.'

At that moment, we were approached by Adam, whose head tilted to one side; he was genuinely crazy. Spittle ran out of the corner of his mouth. He said something that I didn't understand. My father handed him his handkerchief and Adam wiped his mouth and gave it back.

'Tell me, what else did your Flaubert dream about?'
I said.

'He imagined he was sitting in a cage with a lion, the lion had eaten all Flaubert's words and Flaubert wanted to persuade the lion to spit the words out again.'

'And did it spit them out?'

'I assume so, yes.'

'And then?'

'That's it.'

'That's it?'

'Yes,' he stammered, suddenly he was stammering. 'You'll have to forgive me … that's it … it's an embarrassing bit of nonsense …'

The way he was sitting, on the edge of the bench, the way his gaze was roving around, made me realise that all this time, he had actually wanted to say something completely different. He can never say the really important things. He has to use a book as an intermediary. Always. This time though, he can't find one that fits the bill. Flaubert, he's no use. He is ashamed of himself, for prattling on, for the embarrassing bit of nonsense. His gaze roved around and brushed across me and suddenly his despair was evident to me. The whole thing was not a game any more. My heart thumped, and jumped forward a few years – just a quarter of an hour ago I was a child, feeling quietly triumphant about a bicycle race with her father, now that was way back in a childish past. Just one word from me, I thought, one movement from me, and everything returns to the way it was and he remains silent. Or he starts going on about his Flaubert again. I didn't know which I preferred.

'Monika,' he said.

I am getting ahead: we left it there. He had tied himself in knots, and I could not help him, and he could not help himself. What happens to a child if their father decides to bare his soul – or how should I describe something about which I knew nothing? It is like a wrecking ball in action. Afterwards you can no longer say Papa or Vati. I was scared that I would come to despise him. Would I have to call him Josef afterwards? That's how it is when your father says the little word 'I' and really and truly means 'I' with all that entails, you as a child begin to tremble. In his smallness in the convent, he had been bigger. Why does wanting to say 'I' make him small? What he feared was that he would not find another word to follow 'I' – I can find no words now either and found none then. I would have liked to run away from it all, till I dropped from exhaustion. Even the way he said my name put him in a predicament. And me? What about me, now? That I can find no other word than 'predicament' makes me almost sob with helpless- ness; if it was only made of paper, that word, I would scrunch it up and throw it far away from me down a drain. My husband is sitting sorting out his things one floor below, I ring him on my mobile phone and ask: 'Have you ever seen your father crying?' He doesn't even have to think about it. 'No,' he says, 'of course not.' That doesn't help me much. 'Do you want to have a coffee with me?' I ask.

We remember when we were in a flower shop in Lindau, a long time ago now, and we bumped into his father and his lover. At that time, I was still married to my first husband, so we had driven over the border to Lindau, to avoid seeing anyone who knew us. And then we run into his father, just as he's going to buy flowers for his lover. We all introduced ourselves and exchanged pleasantries, in a desultory manner. In the evening his father had rung up and suggested he should come over and see him, there were some things that needed to be discussed.

'What did you discuss?' I ask my husband. 'You never did tell me.'

'Nothing.'

'What do you mean, nothing?'

'He had bought three kilos of vineyard grapes and said they were cheap and had to be eaten or they would just go off.'

My husband's mother was still living then, she was in a care home.

'When,' I ask, 'did you stop calling him Papa and start calling him by his first name?'

'I don't remember any more.'

'From that day on?'

'No, before that.'

What's all this about, asks my husband and I tell him that when I was fifteen or sixteen, no older than that, I was afraid I would lose my father, not through death but because all of a sudden he no longer treated me like his child but more – 'like a friend, a confidante, who you can tell things to that you have not told to anyone else'.

'And?' asks my husband. 'Did he? Did he have a few secrets, too, like my father?'

'Why did you say "a few"?' I ask.

'Because I think, or rather I'm pretty sure, that my father had more than one lover.'

I had not been thinking of the secret or secrets of his father, his and mine are not comparable, mine had no secrets, he definitely did not have a lover, let alone more than one. It wasn't secrets that he wanted to speak to me about and couldn't: it was about taking stock of his life. At the last minute, he realised that I was only fifteen and his daughter, that fifteen is too young and one's own daughter is not the appropriate person to pass judgement on the components of a life.

Twenty-three years later, Vati and I were sitting in the train home from Berlin. After twenty-three years, he once again took up the conversation that had not taken place. On the journey out to Berlin, we had not spoken much to each other: just about the landscape, about the former GDR, how we were looking forward to seeing Renate and excited to find out what she would show us in Berlin. Now on the return journey, he suddenly said: 'Monika.' And I knew there and then we were about to have the conversation that we did not have twenty-three years earlier.

It was not a conversation. I merely listened. He did the talking. And he told me nothing new, no secret, nothing strange, just his life – more or less – that this was the life he'd had but that if he could choose, next time he would pick a different one and that I should not feel hurt, because then I would not have existed, not me nor Renate nor Gretel nor Richard, not even our mother, well she would still have existed, but with a different husband and different children. Berlin had done him so much good! From the first evening when we sat in the gay bar and he had laughed so freely and heartily, like Renate and I had never heard him laugh before. And then during the day – from one antiquarian book-shop to the next, all close to one another, 'perfect for someone with a gammy leg'. He had never been in such a big city in his life. Where there were so many different ways of living. As a recluse or a Gatsby, as a scrounger or a lord, dust from books, dust from the street, dust on one's shoes, dust in one's nose, history and no history, catastrophe and no catastrophe, shops where one could buy white linen boots lined with down for evening wear. Renate and I agree: our father was in heaven.

Back when I was fifteen, no, I could not have imagined this man in a big city.

Then began the time when I disliked everything about him. When I think back, I have the impression that some sort of illness had taken hold of me, that a wave of infection had swept through me. At first, it was only his trousers that irritated me. They were so heavy, even in summer, always the same damned grey with turn-ups, and too long. Then I found myself being driven crazy by his knitted cardigan in that insipid all-over blue. In the end, I was even irritated by the way he breathed in. I would have liked to emigrate to America. I made notes to myself for the compilation of a fictitious curriculum vitae: I would be from Vienna, father an engineer, mother a fashion designer. I wanted to adopt the identity of someone ready to embrace a new age and a new country. I signed up for a course in English and took on various jobs after school, firstly, so that I was at home as little as possible, secondly, to prepare myself for an imminent trip to Chicago. All my friends, both girls and boys, wanted to go to Paris, and if they spoke of America, it was of New York. I wanted to go to Chicago. That was because I had got hooked on the novels of Saul Bellow, first *The Adventures of Augie March*, then *Herzog*, for a long time my favourite book. I passed over the fact that it had been my father who had recommended this author.

And then suddenly it was over. I was healthy. Cured of the anger-illness. He no longer irritated me. I stopped rolling my eyes when he asked me something. I did not get angry with him, I did not pity him, I did not overrate him, I did not underrate him. The way he breathed did not annoy me and I found it easy to agree with him.

I got to know my first husband, moved away from home, married, brought two children into the world, Oliver and Undine, got to know my second husband, got divorced. I seldom visited my father and his wife. We tried our best.

They had already retired, both he and my step-mother, when they gave up the shabby apartment and bought themselves a small house in a nearby village, a mid-terrace house, a small garden at the back with an elderberry bush because an elderberry bush brings good fortune. In the living room, my father had deep shelves fixed to all the free wall space, on each one stood two rows of books, one row in front, one behind to be guessed at if a large book towered over a smaller one. He would have preferred to have had all of them, there were now almost three thousand, arranged around him so that he could always see the spine of each one. The house however did not have a room big enough, and my stepmother had insisted that the other rooms, the bedroom and her sewing room, were to be book-free zones, she didn't want any by the stairs either. My father had given in and reconciled himself, but he was not happy about it. But after the life he'd had, which had dealt him such cruel blows, the two of them settled into a closeness together. He even managed to say as much to me, to Gretel, to Renate and also to her, his wife.

To me he said, unexpectedly and apropos of nothing: 'I like lying beside her and we hold hands.'

I believe I blushed. Which I never do. Although they have two children, my half-sister and my half-brother, I could not conceive of the two of them being intimate. Even as a seven-year-old I had been able to picture tender gestures between him and our Mutti, also the kind that are not done in public, particularly those ones. The ones in public I had seen myself, they had not been sparing with them: holding hands, stroking a cheek, kisses on an eyelid – Mutti's speciality – fond words, teasing; everything soft and secret but still open, everything like a foretaste of what might follow when everyone else was out.

'Why are you telling me that?' I asked him.

'Because you should all know. I don't want you to think you have an unhappy father and an unhappy stepmother.'

He said something similar to my sisters. But he spoke to each of us individually. To speak to the three daughters from his first marriage at the same time, that would have seemed to him too open and exposed. But he knew that we would confide in each other.

Gretel said: 'Things did turn out all right in the end.'

Renate said: 'In reality, we don't know anything at all about him.'

I am inclined to agree with Renate.

After his death, we split the books between us. That was not what he would have wanted, I know. He hoped that they would remain together. My stepmother suggested donating the whole collection to the lending library, I think that would have been more in line with his wishes. But then Renate wanted to have the *Grossen Meyer* encyclopaedia and Gretel the art encyclopaedia, and I did not want to go away empty-handed and said, I would like the *Kindlers Literatur Lexikon*, and so it went on, each one took a chunk. The rest, our stepmother gave to the lending library. But I am getting ahead of myself ...

Word had soon got around the village that a new man had moved in recently who knew a lot about books. The mayor, an upright social democrat, immediately thought to himself that this man would be an ideal candidate for the management of the lending library. My father happily accepted the role, only to discover that the inventory was a huge disappointment. There was not one book that he would have wanted to borrow, not one that he would want to receive as a gift.

At that time, there was a radio programme in Austria called *Quiz in Red-White-Red*, cities and district communities could take part in it, the idea was to find out which area was the most intelligent in the whole country. The mayor applied and his district met the criteria. On one of his visits, the mayor had seen that our father owned the *Grossen Meyer* encyclopaedia, so he asked whether the community could borrow the fifteen volumes, with these one would have a big advantage and might even win the quiz. Our father lent the *Meyer* with a heavy heart. When the books came back, they were so tattered that he could not even bear to handle them. For him, they were ruined, he would have liked to throw them out. The mayor, seeing how unhappy our father was, felt inconsolable too. In order to appease his conscience, he suggested increasing the library stock by means of a hefty increase in budget. Our father was expecting only a slight increase in the paltry sum. But it turned out to be twenty times the original! He asked the mayor, what did he have in mind, what books would be suitable for the readers of the community? The mayor stood up from the kitchen chair and put on his jacket, solemnly declaring:

'You, Herr Helfer, as our keenest and best-qualified reader, should have a free hand in the decision. Choose the books entirely according to your taste and needs. It would be an honour for our community.'

Our father spent long nights thinking about it. His list was extensive and there was not a single book among them in which more than two readers would have been interested, or even one. Only books which interested him.

Soon thereafter, the delivery van arrived, boxes were unloaded, first one, then a second, a third and so on. My father stood there, his hands trembling. He gave the driver everything he had in his wallet as a tip. More than Uncle Walter would have given.

An incredible exhaustion overcame him, and he had to sit down on the floor in the middle of the lending library. He began to slit open the strips of tape on the boxes with a knife. Gradually he piled up books around him, until by the end he was surrounded by a wall of books. He stroked one book after another, sniffed at each one, opened it, removed the dust jacket to see how the spine of the book was designed, looked at the pictures where there were pictures, read a few lines. He spent the whole afternoon like this and the whole evening. The library was closed to visitors that day, it was only open two days in the week. He had been sitting there so long, outside it had started getting dark, when the telephone rang. He propped himself up, tried to stand up, which was not easy with his prosthesis, and hobbled through the mountains of books. He tripped against one pile, it tumbled over and carried him with it. Our father crashed to the floor and was dead. The joy had been too much for him. He was sixty-seven years old.

We all tried our very best.

A Note on the Author and Translator

Monika Helfer grew up in Vorarlberg, Austria. Her novels include the internationally bestselling, Schubart Prize-winning *Die Bagage (Last House Before the Mountain)* and *Löwenherz (Lionheart)*. She has been awarded the Bodensee and Solothurn Literature Prizes, the Johann Beer Prize, and the Austrian Cross of Honor. She lives in Hohenems, Austria.

Gillian Davidson is a literary translator based in London. *Library for the War-Wounded* is the second novel by Monika Helfer that she has translated.

ALSO AVAILABLE FROM MONIKA HELFER

LAST HOUSE BEFORE THE MOUNTAIN

#1 INTERNATIONAL BESTSELLER

THE SPELLBINDING, INTERNATIONALLY BESTSELLING MULTIGENERATIONAL FAMILY STORY

Maria and Josef live with their children in a valley in westernmost Austria. When the First World War breaks out and Josef is drafted into the army, Maria is left to provide for her family alone. Every day is a struggle against starvation, the harsh alpine climate, and the hostile nearby villagers who see Maria as little more than a beautiful temptress out for the men left behind. But when a red-haired stranger arrives in the village, Maria feels happiness seep back into her life and she faces a choice whose consequences will affect the lives of her family for generations to come.

"A poignant, captivating, beautifully woven family saga. As honest as Elena Ferrante, with the folkloric intensity of Téa Obreht, *Last House Before the Mountain* explores the ways we reconstruct our family histories in an attempt to understand who we are." —Christina Baker Kline, #1 *New York Times* bestselling author of *The Exiles*, *A Piece of the World*, and *Orphan Train*

"A master class in literary compression. In just a short span of pages, Helfer brings a whole world of wonder, loss and deep, deep longing to indelible life. How lucky we are that her work is finally available in English." —Laird Hunt, author of National Book Award finalist *Zorrie*